Rae Earl

MY LIFE UPLOADED

【Imprint】
MAKE YOUR MARK

New York

SQUARE
FISH

An imprint of Macmillan Publishing Group, LLC
120 Broadway, New York, NY 10271
fiercereads.com

Square Fish and the Square Fish logo are trademarks of Macmillan and are used by Imprint
under license from Macmillan.

Our books may be purchased in bulk for promotional, educational, or business use. Please
contact your local bookseller or the Macmillan Corporate and Premium Sales Department at
(800) 221-7945 ext. 5442 or by email at MacmillanSpecialMarkets@macmillan.com.

Library of Congress Control Number: 2017957959

ISBN 978-1-250-30908-2 (paperback)   ISBN 978-1-250-13379-3 (ebook)

[Imprint]
MAKE YOUR MARK

@ImprintReads
Originally published in the United States by Imprint
First Square Fish edition, 2020
Book designed by Carol Ly
Square Fish logo designed by Filomena Tuosto
Imprint logo designed by Amanda Spielman

10 9 8 7 6 5 4 3 2 1

This book is protected by the Secret Association of Social Media Felines (SASMF). Stealing/
damaging/folding over the pages of this tome will result in a mandatory visit from specially
trained uniformed commando cats. These felines reserve the right to take control of all your
social media accounts and share what they like.

Even that pic of you in the unicorn outfit. Yes, *that* one. And that baby photo where you hadn't
learned to actually eat. All-over spaghetti is SO NOT a good look.

For Jo-Anne Green.
With thanks for all your
help and your amazing
work with peas.

#RobotWars

You know you've had a bad weekend when your cat is sulking and trying to eat your shoe at the same time. My pet hates me. My phone hates me. My mum's boyfriend hates me.

Things are looking bad right now. But before YOU start hating on me, too, let me try to explain what really happened this afternoon.

Firstly, I am NOT a murderer. I did not try to kill a machine. It was just a simple misunderstanding between a very angry feline, a desk, and my foot. But it all just got completely out of hand, and Mr. Neat Freak and his zombie pack of dusters are exploiting the situation.

And I don't want to blame anyone for the accident, but it WAS Mum's fault. She wanted me to spend the afternoon doing my homework, so she turned the Wi-Fi off. I KNOW. I was forced to find a desperate way to get service so that I could send a message to Lauren. It was an important message that would cheer the gorgeous Laurenmeister up. She's a best friend who is very fed up and in need of some love.

And it should be a simple thing to message your friends. It's a human right but not in this house. This is a mobile dead zone. . . . Not this area. Just my house.

To try to get my message to send, I had to hang out of the window with my arm waving in the air. That didn't work. Our neighbor thought I wanted to speak to her. *There is no problem, Mrs. Milner. I am just living with two unreasonable, controlling dictators.* Then I tried to use the shower in the bathroom as a massive antenna thing. This also failed. The shower is for washing. The shower knew it was not a cell tower and would not play along.

So instead I used my cat, Dave, as a mobile hot spot. I learned some valuable lessons here. A phone will not balance on a cat's back, and the cat will then try to eat the phone in anger. Then it will try to eat the contents of your wardrobe.

Once Dave had deserted me for my socks, I had no choice but to stand on top of my desk, flex my leg, point my toes, and hold my phone up in the air as high as I could. Getting a decent signal to text your best friend should NOT involve ballet, but it was worth trying for Lauren. I was pirouetting by my laptop when Dave decided that she wanted to get involved. There was a huge feline leap with full claw extension onto my knee. I lost my balance and fell off the desk. My heel planted itself firmly on my mum's boyfriend's best friend.

His robot vacuum cleaner. It had come into my bedroom to feed on dust.

As I landed on the machine, it beeped in distress. It stopped eating dirt and switched to a random path of confusion. Dave then attempted to kill the robot vacuum cleaner by jumping on top of it. It did sort of look like an out-of-control pigeon.

At that moment, the neat-freak boyfriend rushes into my bedroom and sees MY cat surfing on top of HIS robot vacuum cleaner. The Neat Freak yells at Dave, then yells at me that I've had it in for him and his "superior cleaning methods" for ages!

He then starts nursing his best vacuum cleaner friend like it's a massive, soppy Labrador, reassuring it that all will be okay. He takes it downstairs, muttering about its delicate microbrush technology, and I haven't seen him since.

So Dave and I are now sitting in my bedroom. I still haven't managed to text Lauren, and I think I am in big trouble. This doesn't seem fair, because I've tried to get along with this man. He's my mum's boyfriend and a neat freak, but I've tried. That's me, I suppose. I try to get along with everyone, because things are just easier that way, aren't they? But you cannot live with a man who puts his relationship with a cleaning device before his relationship with living things.

He's even given the robot vacuum cleaner a name: McWhirter.

And McWhirter follows me everywhere. He's like my rotating, sucking-everything-up shadow. When I eat my toast at breakfast, you hear the Neat Freak saying, "There, boy! Get Millie's crumbs!" When I eat dinner, he's at his master's side. Sitting. Waiting. Staring. I know he's just a machine, but his ON/OFF switch looks like eyes. Glowing, red eyes full of tidiness, hungry for a treat of some of my mess. McWhirter the cleaning robot dog has become my bossy, buzzing stepbrother. He is terrorizing me with his automatic settings and full-view sensor.

He? I'm calling McWhirter *he* now! I can't stay here. I'll go mad. I'll start talking to the dishwasher. Neat Freak does that, too. He hasn't given it a name yet, but it's only a matter of time. He congratulates it when it's finished a cycle.

It's not normal, is it?

All this nonstop trauma over stupid stuff, like fluffy balls on wood floors, makes me think . . .

It makes me think that I need to go live with my dad.

How much twonk can one girl take?! Gary IS a twonk and he gives twonk. Twonks like him do the sort of idiot stuff that HURTS lives. We are not talking *spoon*—meaning the silliness that usually makes you like a person more (LAUREN!). We are talking full-on, drilling-in-your-head, lemon-in-your-eyes-on-a-day-to-day-basis TWONK. It's the WHOLE twonk attitude. They just want to make your life tougher—even when it's tough already. If you're climbing a mountain, they'll come along and say you need a concrete backpack. SERIOUSLY, twonks are WARPED!

I know that sounds a bit "Drama Queen," but I don't seem to belong here anymore. Maybe, if I just move out for a while, Mum might miss me and realize that I'm actually nice to have around. And one great thing about having parents who don't live together is that I actually have somewhere else I could go.

It's *telling* Mum that's going to be SO hard.

My mum isn't evil, but she's strict and tough beyond the belief of any normal human being or even any parent. Living with her is a bit like being in the army without having to wear camouflage trousers or getting the opportunity to squash people you don't like with a tank.

And yes, when I say that, I am thinking of rolling over her boyfriend. And McWhirter.

When it was just Mum and me, we fit together more. I could cope with her rules. Obviously, her turning off the Wi-Fi at eight o'clock EVERY night apart from Saturday wasn't great, but we were at least partners in crime—or *grime*, as the Neat Freak called it when he first arrived with his stupid Lycra shorts and power mop. No, Mum didn't clean much and there was an inch of furry-based mess on top of the widescreen—but who cares?

She works at the hospital. She's not a surgeon or anything, but she has to order all the swabs and bandages. So she's basically responsible for stopping people from bleeding to death on a national scale. She saves lives! She doesn't need to DUST. And she doesn't want me cleaning too much, either. She doesn't want me to become tied to an oven, baking my signature-style Black Forest gâteau for some man. She would much rather I come with her to her boxercise class or do my homework or BOTH. At the same time. Mum does multi-tasking like no other woman dares.

I haven't got a signature-style cake, by the way—mainly because Mum and I aren't big on baking. Mum says that if you can get a perfectly decent apple pie from the supermarket, then why bother spending two hours making one? Just watch people do it on TV. I agree. We agree on most things. Or we did until Gary turned up and hoovered all our love away.

Gary. Gary "Neat Freak" Woolton.

Do you know that only twenty-three babies in the WHOLE of this country have been called Gary in the past two years?! This is because Garys CAUSE TROUBLE. And they polish everything at the same time.

Every Friday, Mum and I used to slum it together on the sofa in our pajamas and watch television till one in the morning. Now Friday night for me is YouTube on my own, and Friday night for her is date night with a man who smells like Pine-Sol. I can't even watch Netflix, because they're always too busy watching something about the Tudors. He's ruined everything.

And since I've been back at school, Mum's insisting that I start following a strict study plan. My final exams aren't until JUNE. And don't even get me started on Gary's cleaning schedule. The oven does not need daily cleaning. Before he came along, we hardly used it.

I have to get out of here. Especially now that Gary thinks I'm a robot vacuum cleaner murderer. It's for Dave's protection as much as mine. Even if it's just for a few months. That's all. Nothing too drastic.

I need to think about how to tell Mum that I want to go live at Dad's, though. But my phone is beeping like mad. Finally, I've got a signal. Oh. It's Lauren. It's . . .

Oh no.

No. No. NO!

It's . . .

This isn't good. Oh prawning HELL.

I need to get over there. Trust me. This is bad. BAD. Everything about me can wait. Lauren is in TROUBLE. THIS could go viral.

#StyleShamed

Lauren's mum lets me straight in. She likes me. She thinks I'm a "good influence." This is because I make Lauren live on Planet Earth for at least some part of the day. The rest of the time, Lauren is on Planet Lauren. It's a fantastic place to be, but lots of adults seem to struggle with it. I love it, though. She's the opposite of me. She does, THEN she thinks.

There's no sign of Lauren's dad, which is probably why her mum is looking so cheerful. Lauren's parents don't get on. They're a soap without the funny bits.

When I get to Lauren's bedroom, she's under her duvet like a very shy and sad quilted tortoise. I can hear her sniffling.

"Go away," she moans until she realizes that it's me.

She pokes her head out. "Oh, Mills—it was just terrible. Unbelievable. Remember those new heels? My first proper pair? You said . . ."

I know what I said. I tried them on, too, and I said they should come with crutches, because breaking your ankle was almost guaranteed.

"Oh no, Lauren. Have you hurt yourself?" I say to her. "They

7

are hard, Lauren. It's like balancing on really drunk giraffes. The struggle is REAL."

"I know. So I thought I'd practice just by walking to the store. It's only three minutes away in normal shoes. Actually, it was more like twenty in these heels, but . . . I was doing okay until I had to go up the curb, and then . . ." Lauren pops back into her blanket shell. "I heard giggling. I think someone might have been"—Lauren gulps—"following me. What if it's Mr. Style Shame?"

The Mr. Style Shame Instagram account has a massive number of followers. We don't know who runs it, but he's a big name around here. His logo is an outline of a guy wearing dark glasses. He's probably some Batman genius who lives in a bitter den of sass. People WE KNOW have been featured by him. He is constantly on the prowl, like a fashion lion, hunting for people who aren't looking their best. THEN he pounces. And his attacks are FATAL. He blurs your face, but everyone at school still knows who you are, and no—the adults can't stop him. They've got NO idea. They think life begins and ends with Facebook.

If you're unlucky enough to be featured, there's a very good chance that you could be in an online-sensation nightmare in under an hour.

And now he may have a photo of my beautiful best friend falling over in a pair of pink stilettos while carrying a can of Sprite and a Kit Kat. You see what I mean? This isn't good. And Lauren knows it.

"Take a look for me, Mills. See if I'm on there."

I pick up my phone and—yes, of course I follow Mr. Style Shame. Don't hate me. We all do. You need to check to make sure you're not on there. He can strike at any time and . . .

Yes. Sure enough, there is a photo of my beautiful best friend in

8

midair with a filter to maximize her completely wonky, going-all-over-the-place body. One very pink high heel is in the gutter. The other one is flying beside Lauren's shoulder like a very embarrassed parrot.

If the photo wasn't bad enough, he's written:

> Look at this modern-day Cinderella leaving her glass slippers behind! Remember: If you're going for #Glam, practice first, girls, or you're very unlikely to find your own Prince Charming. #Fail #Heels #Mr.StyleShame

"Is it there?" Lauren whispers.

"Er . . . yes."

"How many likes?"

Do I lie?

I take several hundred likes off the actual figure before telling her.

Lauren pulls the duvet so far over her head that she looks like she may be planning to hibernate forever. I think she's trying really hard not to cry. Her face collapses when she's upset and doesn't want me to see. When she sobs, I sob. That's how we are.

I hate this. Lauren is my BFF—one of the sweetest, loveliest people you will ever, EVER meet. And Mr. Style Shame makes so many people feel totally, trollingly BLURGH about themselves. He does that CLASSIC evil thing of pretending to be funny so he can get away with it. I'm sick of him.

But right now, I need to work out a way to make my best friend feel better.

And I think I have an idea.

#BearEyes

If there are two things my best friend loves, it's makeup and our favorite vloggers. We both love them. Vlogging just cheers you up, doesn't it? And our faves are always THERE—during the daytime or at 2:00 a.m. when you can't sleep because you've got something on your mind.

"Come on, Lozza," I say. I can feel her sobbing under the duvet. "He'll find a new victim in the next five minutes. You'll be forgotten by Monday."

I don't actually believe that, but I just want to make her feel better. People are still talking about Holly Graham's skirt-tucked-in-striped-underpants Mr. Style Shame tragedy, but Lauren doesn't need to hear that right now.

"Let's watch Bella Fruity—the inexpensive beauty—and do some serious eyes."

Bella is one of our favorite vloggers. She does SERIOUSLY low-budget but highly magnificent makeovers. We have nearly worn YouTube out watching her genius with eyes. We have tried her exotic-bird eye makeup, her showgirl brows, her Kardashian contouring, AND her Kate Middleton wedding makeup tutorials. After that, we

10

could have basically married Prince William. We looked bride-aliciously fabulous.

Today, though, I think we should keep it simple, so I say to Lauren, "Let's do Bella's perfecto winged cateye look."

Lauren finally comes out of her covers, and we do our makeup. She puts hers on brilliantly, but, just to make her laugh, I get hold of the foundation and liquid eyeliner, pick up my phone, and hit RECORD. . . .

"Okay. So today we are going for the panda look. A lot of you contact me and say, 'Millie, I want to look like a big furry bear in a zoo.' So what do you do? It's EASY. First of all, just get some foundation that's about five shades lighter than your actual skin tone. SMEAR it all over your face and then get some black liquid eyeliner and draw MASSIVE BLACK CIRCLES ALL OVER YOUR EYES. Now just grab a potted plant or some broccoli from the fridge, stick it in your mouth, and—BINGO!—you're a panda! NOW, EAT THAT, BELLA FRUITY. I'm the BIG BEAR PANDA BEAUTY! I could go to any party at any zoo in the world."

Lauren is howling with laughter behind me.

"Who cares what you look like?! Who cares if you trip over? If your BFF is upset because she thinks someone caught her looking stupid, just do something completely spoon like this to remind her that none of us are perfect. Also, there is no shame in trying something new, but there is shame in making people or bears feel bad about themselves. So THANK YOU."

I'm on an emergency goofball mission here, and it's worked. Lauren is laughing wildly. Going full silly to cheer up Lauren is totally worth it.

"Now I'm going to upload that. No one will care about your fall if they see THIS!"

Normally, I'd never do anything like this. Most photos or videos I share online are thought about, shot at least thirty times, and put through a really good filter. BUT, as Aunty Teresa says, desperate times call for desperate measures. My BFF needs the love.

And I do it! To be honest, I've got hardly any views on any of my stuff, so I don't think anyone will see it. Also, I'm not sure it's going to stop people talking about Lauren's spectacular fall, but it's worth doing it to show her that I'm WITH her. You'd do the same. I don't mind doing really silly stuff if I'M in actual control of it.

Then Lauren says something really lovely. "You always cheer me up, Mills. You always know what to do."

I sometimes do. I'm good at sorting things out for other people, like Lauren and Aunty Teresa. What I'm not so good at is sorting out my own life, like how to tell Mum I want to go live with my dad because her boyfriend is the most annoying person on this earth.

"Millie," says Lauren. "Thank you. But do you want to take off your panda makeup now? It's quite difficult to take pandas seriously."

She's right. Pandas are not good at discussing who they would like to live with, as they mainly live in zoos with one partner. In fact, pandas are very lucky when you think about it. I bet no one comes in and cleans up their bamboo with a portable dustbuster, GARY.

"You're right, Loz. I need to look professional. Dave tried to kill McWhirter, and I've had enough. I'm going to tell Mum that I want to go and live with Dad for a bit."

Lauren looks taken aback. "Millie! Why do you want to leave

your mum?! You two are like sisters, really, but sisters that get on! I know the Neat Freak is a bit—"

This makes me cross. "Gary is not 'a bit' anything. He is a FULL-ON pain. And Mum obviously doesn't want me there unless I'm doing school stuff. It would only be for a little while. . . ."

Lauren looks at me and then softly says, "Millie, are you sure you're not just being a little . . . jealous like a spoiled only-child? Your mum deserves to be—"

I lose it slightly. "Lauren, this isn't about Mum being happy. It's about her deciding that a man who uses hospital-grade hand sanitizer as shower gel is the ONE."

Lauren backs down and changes the subject.

"By the way"—she now has her duvet wrapped around herself like some kind of very warm poncho—"have you seen the new boy?"

Have I seen the new boy? Yes, of course I have. New people at school are interesting. We know Reuben Stubbs can still fold himself up into a locker. It used to be impressive, but we've seen the same trick a hundred times now. Anyone NEW is a very good thing.

Lauren looks very proud of herself. "I have information on the man!" She attempts a swagger. "He's called Danny Trudeau, and he is Canadian."

"Ohhh . . ." I put on our MAJOR GOSSIP ALERT voice. "Is he? How did HE end up HERE?"

Lauren starts to whisper. "Well. The rumor is that he could be related to"—Lauren looks around to check that there aren't any other people listening—"the president."

"The president of what?" I ask her. It sounds like a film.

"I don't know," Lauren says before realizing she sounds ever so slightly ridiculous and crumpling into a giggly mess on the floor.

"LOZZA!" I throw a hamburger pillow at her.

Lauren gets up and angrily slams the hamburger down on the bed so hard that it loses its bun. "Now, guess who's already following him on Instagram!"

We both know: Erin Breeler.

How can I explain her?

Erin Breeler is the queen of Instagram at school. She is guaranteed hundreds of likes on everything she posts. She could put a pic up of her avocado salad and get total adoration from every breathing thing on this earth. Even non-breathing things, like the avocados, would probably like her posts.

On her account, she has the most perfect photos of her totally amazing, glowing life. Selfies like you've never seen. Her angles are perfect. Her eyebrows are sculpted. HER BUM IS A CELEBRITY ON ITS OWN. She smiles with perfect teeth (even when she had braces, she looked unbelievable) and wears clothes that the rest of us don't dare to. She does yoga poses in jeans. It looks GREAT. You think I'm exaggerating? Go and look. The girl is phenomenal.

And even though it's all about what she looks like on the outside, she writes stuff like *Feel the inner glow radiate out* and *I can be more mindful in this mohair cardigan*, so you can't even call her shallow.

She's really clever about what she posts. When she had a zit, she made it into a good thing. She put her little finger over it, puckered her lips, and posed with a *No apologies! No one is perfect!* caption. She acts like she doesn't really know what she's doing, and everybody falls for it. It's so FALSE, but everyone seems to love her.

Girls like Erin don't hang around with girls like Lauren and me. She's too cool. Too edgy. And if you get in her space, she will take you down in SUCH a whip-smart way. Yet, a weird part of me still wants her to like me.

I know—pathetic. And, honestly, I'm scared of her. And I hate that in myself. She's superconfident, both at school and in her posts, and it's like—

"Millie! Come back to the room!" Lauren is calling out to me.

"Sorry," I say. "I was just thinking about Erin Breeler. Beautiful people can make you drift off, can't they? Erin and Danny. Lovely Danny with his lovely—"

"Bag!" Lauren interrupts. "Have you seen it, Millie? That boy has serious stationery."

Lauren likes paper and pens more than anything. She has a Pinterest board that is just fluorescent markers.

"I was going to say his eyes, but anyway, Loz, I'd better go."

Lauren gives me a huge hug. She also wishes me luck, which I'm going to need.

The truth is, I could stay here forever.

I feel sick. I don't want to go home.

#FamilyMatters

When I get home, Mum still isn't back from the big weekly Saturday shop. Gary is cleaning the toaster and telling it off for hoarding little bits of bread. This is normal. He has a feud with the toaster. He says it's a bad design. The toaster feels the same way about Gary but cannot talk.

Actually, I don't think Gary is speaking to me after I damaged his robotic true love. He looks up when I come in but then goes back to cleaning. Who spends their weekend doing that? Someone with no friends who likes telling things off. Worryingly, there is no sign of McWhirter.

I go upstairs to my bedroom, and Dave comes and joins me. We are refugees from Gary "Neat Freak" Woolton's Democratic Republic of Clean. I create crumbs. Dave sheds hair. We are the enemy.

I keep thinking about what Mum is going to say when I tell her about Dad's. I can't decide if she'll be relieved or calm or . . .

She's going to be cross. Who am I kidding? I try to take my mind off things. What will my new video thumbnail be? A screenshot of something I've watched? A photo I've taken? Mum's furious, sobbing face?

Finally, I hear her coming through the front door. I take Dave downstairs. Mum is in the kitchen, flustered, and loaded with bags from Sainsbury's. A soggy baguette is poking out of one of them, and wet carbs always put her in a REALLY foul mood.

I know I should probably wait for her to take her coat off and try to have a proper, sensible chat, but ALL the feelings EVER are rushing up from deep inside of me. I end up yelling at her so loudly that Dave the cat leaps into the air—so high that, if I'd been filming it, the video would have been a YouTube sensation: "SuperCat Scales a Building!"

"Mum! I want to go and live with Dad."

Mum just carries on unpacking. She must have heard, but I try again just in case.

"Mum—I want to go and live with Dad! At Granddad's house. It's a REAL place. It has a roof. It's FINE!"

This has been building up all summer, so surely it can't come as a surprise.

Mum wraps the soggy baguette in a tea towel, hands it to Gary, and says, very calmly, "Of course you do, Mills. It's like the Wild West over at your granddad's. Your granddad tries, but you know what your dad is like. And don't get me started on Teresa. You'd be able to do what you like, but you're perfectly okay here. I know you think some of my rules are over the top, but turning the Wi-Fi off at night means your brain gets a rest! I'm looking after you! Protecting you! Now, stop being silly and tell me what's really wrong."

This makes me cross. How could she not have noticed how unhappy Gary has been making me? I try to take a deep breath, but my brain goes on heavy-rain-flood mode and my mouth gushes out all sorts of horror.

"Because, Mum, eating a custard cream in this house has become a five-stage process involving a dustpan and brush. And you DO NOT need a side plate to eat a banana! A banana is a big, solid mass. It has its own neat little container—its actual skin! It's the most interior design–friendly fruit known to man. It loves being clean. Why are we even discussing how tidy food naturally is? See what Gary's done to us?! And stop staring at my hand."

I realize I've picked up a banana and am banging it up and down to back up every point I'm making. Fruit torture is not a good look.

Mum says, "You're going to bruise that, Millie."

Gary is already brandishing a newspaper just in case I make the banana fully mushy and he has to wrap it up for the bin. He can't help himself. He then starts pretending this argument is not happening and begins what he would call a "light clean" of the kitchen units.

I don't care. I am on a serious rant.

"Mum, I didn't mind your study schedules or your stupid rules. Mostly, I can put up with them! BUT NO ONE CAN LIVE LIKE THIS. We used to have great times together. Now we NEVER do. You've changed. And you've always said, 'Don't change for anyone. Don't change for a man.' But that is exactly what you've done. You call yourself a feminist? You're actually a sappy-dappy cheeseball love lady. You're not my mum anymore. You're HIS gooey girlfriend!" I point at Gary, who has frozen midpolish. "And you don't let me decide stuff for myself, like when I do my homework or how late I stay at Lauren's, even though I never do anything wrong. I don't ever get to do anything my way. It always has to be your way, and it isn't fair."

All this is terrible, but it's how I feel.

Gary "Neat Freak" Woolton, who is NOT my dad, shouts, "Go to your room!"

Mum, who is still my mum, says quietly, "What's happened to my lovely, sensible, clever girl?"

I yell, "She's in a . . . a coma of really fed-up!" Which is a totally rubbish response, but I'm really angry.

When I storm out of the room, I trip over McWhirter, who is probably trying to escape all the noise. It completely ruins my exit, but at least he is still alive. My aunty Teresa would call this karma. I call it further evidence of my life being ruined by cleaning equipment—vacuum sabotage. I bet Gary programmed him that way.

#NotADiva

Are you still here? I'm surprised. I'm a bit horrible. I'm sorry you had to witness that.

I curl up on my bed and have a mini cry—a wrong-time-of-the-month sort of sob at a sad film. I can see that Mum loves Gary. The calm part of my brain can see that he makes her laugh, and he rubs her dry heels with cocoa butter. She'd been single for years because she didn't want to settle for second-best. Gary came along with his posh mountain bike and amazingly expensive muesli and—BANG!—it was major relationship time. So believe me—I don't want to ruin my mum's happiness.

But if I'm honest, the whole situation is making *me* really unhappy. This house feels like a ride at a theme park that never stops, and I can't get off. And it's not making me feel good. My chest feels tight. And the thing is, in that argument with Mum, I didn't even sound like me. I'm usually totally chill and . . .

Okay, let's just say it: *sensible*.

It's a CURSE. I've always been that way. I blame Mrs. Woods. She wrote in my school report: *Millie is a girl with plenty of common sense.* How did she know? Well, when Stephen Pearson broke his arm while running around on the playground, pretending to be an owl, I was the one who suggested that we should probably call an ambulance. Everyone else was trying to find a phone to get a photo. Including, probably, Mrs. Woods.

I was nine.

I know. Sweet. But also a bit tragic.

You can be anything at school—geeky with geek chic, a cosplayer, or a MAJOR member of the Nerdverse—that's basically ALL FINE. No one cares. Bradley Sanderson in the year above has a vlog chann called The King of Elevation, where he films himself in lifts or going up and down escalators. One of his videos has seventy-seven thousand views! That's way more than Erin has ever got for one of her mindful-in-mohair posts. To some people—admittedly not many at school—HE is the BOMB.

But me? Being the sort of person that is quite . . . wise? Well, I'm less cool than Daniel Gyver from tenth grade, who can chew through six entire pens in one geography lesson, including the metal nibs.

My friends love me. Mum says I've got a good ear and a soft shoulder. She doesn't mean I've got a floppy, mushy body (sorry—you probably realized that). She means I usually know what to do in a crisis. Even the sort of crisis that Lauren says makes you hide in your bedroom for days eating crisps and playing *Pet Doctor*.

I can usually cope with my weird family. I can even cope with real men. I've had a REAL BOYFRIEND—Dylan Anthony. Yes! Him! HE was mine. For a month and a half. Until we had a massive row over the suffragettes. He thought they were overreacting. I said not being allowed to vote JUST because you're a girl was a pretty big deal.

I know. I sound like a right doofus. But in that moment, it just felt RIGHT. This is why I feel so panicky now. I'm not normally the one having a meltdown. I'm not the one who makes any silly decisions, and yet, here I am about to. . . .

It is *not* sensible to want to leave your mum and go live with a man who still lives with his own dad at the age of thirty-eight and who once used elastic bands and a copy of *Top Gear* magazine to make you a diaper.

There is not much common sense there, Mrs. Woods. But this is what I want to do.

Perhaps I just need time—some time to stop being a wobbling mess. I'm not a dessert shaking in a desert. I'm Millie. I'm . . .

I need to go.

For once, I'm going to follow my heart, and my head can just . . . shut up, be quiet, and DISAPPEAR. If it possibly can. And if it can't, my heart can go out partying alone and my brain can stay home with a tub of ice cream and watch a film.

I must be nervous. Can't stop thinking of desserts. CLASSIC sign.

#Heartache

After some mumbling downstairs, Mum comes up to see
me. She's in tough mode. I can tell because her eye is twitching.
This happens to both of us when we are angry. It's a stupid genetic
trait we share.

"Mills," she says, sitting next to me on my bed.

Sitting next to me. You'll recognize that as a brilliant parent
tactic that's meant to say, *I'm on your level. I understand.*

I don't think she does.

"I understand that it's difficult to share me with Gary. . . ."

She definitely doesn't understand.

"You're not a tube of Pringles, Mum!"

"No—but you're used to having me to yourself. And now I've
got someone else to focus on."

I'm quite calm now. "Someone else," I say, "who has completely
insane levels of cleanliness. He tried to use an antiseptic wipe on a
cushion the other day—"

"He struggles with Dave. He's never had pets," Mum interrupts.

"Whatever, Mum. Dave cleans herself at least twice a day. She
would probably use deodorant if they made it paw-friendly."

I'm still calm. Ish.

"Millie," Mum whispers, putting her arm around me. "You're right. Dave is a very clean cat. And you are a good girl. You're self-regulating . . ." (What does this mean? She's always saying it!) "When you were a toddler, you would ask to go to bed. You've always been . . ."

We cuckoo together like Granddad's tacky clock: "Sensible."

"I've rung your dad. He's really happy to have you. And he says you can bring Dave—but, Millie, I don't want you to go! I won't stop you if that's what you REALLY want, but in that magnificent head and heart of yours, I know *you know* that this is a bad idea. You're back at school. You need stability. You know you do!"

How does Mum do it?! She sees straight into the heart of me like a drone with a really clever missile. And she carries on. She can read me like a book that has hardly any words and lots of pictures.

"Perhaps we can work together and find a compromise to stop all this? How about if the Wi-Fi goes off at ten o'clock and if we all, as a family, have a conference about crumbs?"

This makes me smile even though I don't want to. I put my head down so Mum can't see. I know she's trying to make me laugh.

"You know," Mum says softly, "Gary is a lovely guy. Yes, he's very house-proud, but he also makes me laugh a lot. He's funny, Millie. Give him a chance."

I don't believe this for one minute. The Neat Freak is probably already planning to turn my bedroom into a Museum of Sanitation (that's a good word stolen from the hand dryers at school) to display his collection of SERIOUS dusters.

"Come on, Millie." Mum squeezes my shoulders. "You know I just want the best for my little girl."

And THAT is the problem. To Mum, I am still that little girl in a doctor costume trying to wrap Dave's ear with a dishcloth. She won't let me actually become an adult. Moving out is really the only way to show her and Gary that I AM one. Or nearly am one.

I snuggle into her shoulder. "Mum, I love you, but I really want to go and live with Dad. Just for a bit. I think some time away from here will be good for me."

Mum looks hurt but keeps her arm around me. She takes a deep breath.

"Okay. Well, I don't want you to go. Even for a little while," Mum says. "But you'll only be down the road. And I know that, whatever I might say, you're a big girl, really. I'm not going to stop you if that's what you *really* want to do. Perhaps you'll appreciate what you have here, and you'll come back. . . ."

She stops talking and sadly plods out of my room. I hear her sniff. Please let it be a sudden allergy to pet hair and not tears.

Oh, Mum! I want to stay. I want HIM to go. IT IS HIM! I don't mind your rules, homework, or even the way you tell me I shouldn't have a boyfriend till I'm thirty-two. I just want him to go and for you to let me be normal and live in the twenty-first century.

But I don't say that. I text Lauren to tell her what's happened. Then I go downstairs to tell Mum that I'll pack some overnight stuff and my school uniform and come back for the rest next weekend. I don't speak to Gary. Thanks, head, for still being a little bit my boss.

I think.

Before I go and put my things in the car, I take a photo of my room and put it on Instagram. All my books, and my lights shaped like cacti. With a Slumber filter, it looks really cool. It also means I can check in the future to see if anyone has moved anything or tried to scrub it. Don't mess with me, Gary. I am basically a forensic policewoman scientist thingy, and I can trace your every cleaning move.

By the time I leave home, my post already has a couple of likes. I'm collecting witnesses. AND they like the way I've done my room!

My old room.

What am I doing? Brain, come back from holiday. I'm going to live with my dad.

#My Fam

As Mum and I drive to Granddad's, I think about what's just happened. Mum's car is a good place to think. She drives like a granny and keeps within the speed limit even when there isn't a sign or a safety camera. I can turn off reality and overthink things.

Yes. This has been very . . . *civilized*, really. That's the word to use when everyone behaves themselves and acts in a way that won't get them on daytime telly yelling at each other. My family is like that, really. We have slightly barking streaks of loon (Aunty Teresa), but mainly "the team works," as Dad says. This is because:

@parents:

My parents are divorced but in the loveliest way possible. Dad and Mum met in Ibiza when they were partying 24/7. Mum used to wear neon bikinis and cowboy hats. But after I turned four, Mum and I came back here for school. Dad stayed in Spain and ran a club, then a tapas bar, and then a bungee-jumping business. He came back a year ago and is still looking for something permanent, so he lives with Granddad. Mum and Dad still seem to really like each other—they just don't want to live with each other. I know! It's really unusual, but it's good for me. Dad seems to understand how difficult it is to be my age. I think Mum has forgotten. And Gary Woolton was never young at all. I bet he's never even been to a party. Except maybe to clean up afterward.

@Granddad:

Granddad is my dad's dad and is basically okay. He's a massive sexist. This is because he was born practically before feminism was actually invented. BUT he loves me and sort of doesn't think of me as a girl. He always says, "You're different from most women, Millie. You don't nag, you don't cry, and you don't shout at me for having muddy fingernails." This is shocking, and you'll be thinking, *How do you even deal with that man?* Look—you just have to remember that he's ancient and that occasionally he gives me five pounds from his pension money to buy something nice. HA!

@AuntyTeresa:

Aunty Teresa is La Diva Loca. She got this nickname from a Spanish man called Juan she was engaged to until she found out he was married to someone else from Estonia. She is SO unlucky with guys *and* work, so she lives with my granddad, too. Occasionally. She's also lived in a garage, in her friend's conservatory for six months, and even in a tent in a field near Glastonbury. She thought that if she pitched up there and lived off the land, she'd eventually get free entry to the festival.

She lasted five days and made herself ill eating poisonous berries. I've basically looked after her since I was born, even though she is twenty-four years older than me. At a job interview once, they asked her if she had any questions and she said, "What's the best way to get rid of verrucas?" You see—I have to be sensible, as a lot of the so-called adults around me are not.

@Dave:

Dave the cat is actually a girl. Don't ask. I was three. My mum asked me what I'd like to call her, and I said Dave. It's the stupidest thing I've done, but it sort of suits her. She's a feline rebel who lives on the edge. Actually, she mainly just sleeps and tries to pinch your crisps, but she's my cat, and we understand each other.

So things were working okay until Gary came along. I lived with Mum, and we would go to Granddad's every week for Sunday lunch and after school on Fridays. But now I'm going to Granddad's for much more than that. I just need to look on the positive side of all of this: no more iron rules, no more set bedtimes, no more homework times, no more Gary following me around with a dustpan and brush and a can of furniture polish . . .

Oh, why do I feel so . . . nervous? I keep getting this feeling in my tummy like a knot. A big lump of worry.

Dave is not happy inside the cat carrier. She looks very grumpy. Cages don't fit with her rebel credentials. I tickle her chin through the grate. She pushes all her gray tabby fur through the wire and does a massive tuna-breath hiss at me. I have to be strong. For Dave. She's going to miss the hedge where she waits for wild-bird burgers.

Come on, Millie. Pull it together.

That's me talking to me, by the way. Dave can't talk. Yet.

#GlowStickDad

When we get to Granddad's, Dad is GLOWING. I've made his Saturday night—and probably his life—complete. He gives me a huge hug and says, "MILLS! You've come to live with lads who love you. We are going to have so much FUN! I've made your bedroom up. Pop upstairs and put your stuff down."

Mum stands at the front door, looking sad. The outside security light makes her look like a *Doctor Who* villain. She is not. She is lovely. I see her mouth, *Look after her*, at Dad.

Dad mouths back, *Of course I will.*

I say good-bye to Mum and she says something, but no one can hear anything because Dave is howling to be let out. It sounds like she's in pain, but she's not. She is having a major tantrum. By the time I've stuck my finger in to rub her head (she bites it), Mum has gone.

Luckily, Granddad arrives with a hot piece of chicken and gives Dave a gourmet snack with one of his supercrinkly old fingers. Dave goes to purr factor ten and shuts up. Granddad also gives me a piece and whispers, "Roast meat makes everything on earth happy."

I think the chicken would disagree, but now is not the time to go vegetarian. Granddad hugs me, and I go upstairs with Dave.

Dad has done quite a good job on my new room. He has moved his bongo drums and taken out most of Aunty Teresa's junk. There's still her collection of cuddly toys and Sylvanian Families, though. If you move those things, she'll go into full panic mode and have to breathe into a bag. I've seen it.

So there are miniature rabbits and a massive Winnie the Pooh, but I notice that there's no actual clothing rack. "Dad—where can I put my school uniform and stuff?"

"Well, I thought you could hang it over Aunty Teresa's exercise bike. She got it on eBay during a New Year's sale and was going to use it every day for half an hour during *Hollyoaks*, but she never got around to it. It's not forever—just till we . . . till we . . . get you something . . . more appropriate. Anyway, settle yourself in, Lady Mills. I'll go and finish tea. Will the usual Dad special be okay?"

I tell him it will be fine.

It isn't really, but he looks so happy that I don't want to make a fuss or make him feel bad.

I put my jeans over the exercise bike, take a photo, share it, and write:

Sometimes you have to make the best of what you have. Even if that means you have to make exercise equipment into a wardrobe. #Fail

Dad won't mind. He understands the banter. No one will see it anyway. I'm not Erin Breeler. I haven't got worldwide followers hanging on my every word.

What I have got is chips and mayonnaise with a veggie coulis waiting for me. Not #Glam but #MyFam.

#LikeAvalanche

When I check my phone after my tea, I get a bit of a shock. The first thing I see is a message from Lauren.

> Mills. Massive post! What's your dad's place like? x

It's unbelievable that, in under an hour, a stupid post about an abandoned bike that was bought in a panic from an eBay New Year's sale has had some shares and LOADS of likes! Plus, I've got thirty-two new followers. And it's quite late and the Wi-Fi is still on! Coming here was the right decision! For now. This is all the savory-stuffing-balls of amazing.

Just as I'm scrolling through all the comments (*My mum uses her mini trampoline as a shoe rack!*), Lauren calls me.

"Have you seen? Have you seen?!" she is screeching out of the phone.

"Yeah," I say. "It was only a stupid thing about my dad's place. It's not—"

"But, Millie—you're funny loads of the time, and you notice things that other people don't. Look how often you make things better by making me smile. You NEVER fail. And Gracie messaged me. Her sister is in tenth grade and was talking about you! Apparently, loads of them are dying at the panda thing that you did to cheer me up. They've shared it everywhere! You're just GOOD. Honestly, I think you should do a proper vlog or something! Not Instagram, 'cause that's Erin's, but a vlog!"

"Come on, Lauren. I'm not that interesting. I'm not, like"—and this is the first person who leaps into my mind—"the Mad Baltic Boy Scientist and his dangerous slime baths."

"But you could be! Sort of. I mean, you're not a boy, and I don't think you should do vlogs involving kiddie pools and explosives. But. Seriously. I know other people would totally love you. You could do it from your bedroom. You could start off by talking about how to deal with insane aunties and their exercise bikes. . . . Just try it! YOLO!"

YOLO. You only live once. It's Lauren's favorite phrase. She uses it whenever she wants me to do something a bit brave or out of the ordinary. I'm not always so good at doing this. Because . . . all right, I'll tell you. But PLEASE don't think I'm being boring, or . . .

#YOLOSBC

I'm going to be dead honest with you. I'm a bit of a worrier. It's why I'm on the more . . . what does Mum call it? The *cautious* side.

I think it might have started when Mum got run over when I was six. She broke her pelvis and was in the hospital for ages. I don't remember a lot of it, but I do remember seeing her in plaster up to her actual face and thinking, *Oh, don't leave me, Mum.* It just seems like the world is a really dangerous place. And when you google stuff, it gets worse. Six hundred fifty thousand car accidents a year are caused by random insects. A plane once crashed because of some wasps in a tiny tube. There's a jellyfish the size of a fingernail that can kill you! Okay, it's very unlikely for jellyfish to be in Devon, where we normally go on holiday, but still! Stepladders, scarves, lawnmowers, cows! All these things have caused serious injuries, you know.

I'd better not google "accidents caused by exercise bikes." That'll be another thing to worry about.

Granddad gets it. He seems to see through me. He says Grandma was like this, too. "The Swan," he called her. She looked graceful on the outside, but underneath, where no one could see, she was paddling furiously. Mum gets it, too. Or used to, before Gary.

So, YES, Lauren. You only live once. So be careful.

This is why I like my bedroom so much. You've got friends on Messenger and you've got people on YouTube who just want to make you laugh or help you put your lippy and blusher on the right way. AND you've got people who seem quite happy to jump into frozen lakes dressed as lizards to promote their band. You can watch other people do the risky stuff. I CAN STAY SAFE.

Who am I kidding? Your bedroom is also the place where trolls can say what they like about you. Or where you can see the photos Mr. Style Shame has posted of you looking like a massive spoon.

Perhaps Lauren is right. Perhaps I should start #YOLOing and just GO FOR IT. I've broken free from Mum and the Neat Freak. Perhaps I *am* braver than I thought. Better than I thought. And being a panda to cheer up Lauren was pretty epic. Perhaps I should just do a vlog. Instagram is great, but with a vlog you can TALK to people. Have a laugh. Perhaps I should just put the camera on now and just . . . just . . .

What?

What sort of stuff would I talk about? I can't talk about fashion or beauty—and, anyway, hundreds of vloggers are already doing it way better than me. Could I pretend to be an animal other than a panda? Maybe my specialty is just comedic bears.

Dave is looking at me. Right now, I think she'd make a better vlogger than me, and she's currently trying to attack my cardigan and eat her own tail at the same time.

#GrumpyCat

When I wake up, I realize the following:

1. I've had the worst night's sleep ever, mainly because I kept checking my phone every five minutes. I now have 1,086 likes on my bike photo and 859 views of the panda vlog. This is what it must feel like to be Erin Breeler. It's good. I like it.

2. I am wearing Aunty Teresa's Christmas pudding beanie because this is actually a fridge pretending to be a house.

3. Dave is staring at me from the end of the bed.

4. Lauren is also staring at me from the end of the bed.

"Who let you in?" I love my friends, but I don't expect them to actually be under the duvet with me on a Sunday morning.

"Er . . . no one," Lauren whispers. "I just let myself in."

I should have remembered. This is not Mum's house, with its supersensitive burglar alarm and multiple locks. This is Granddad's house; there might as well be a massive human cat flap where the front door is.

Lauren is giving me her full-on serious face. She looks like an aye-aye lemur—cute but slightly terrifying.

"Mills. This is . . . this is . . . right . . . this is . . ."

"This is what, Loz?"

Lauren's cheeks twitch because her face is allergic to being sensible. If eyebrows could do Pilates . . . I'm expecting something life-changing, because she looks like she's about to burst.

"This is a bit epic, Mills. TITANIC."

And then she makes a movement with her hands like something has exploded in a microwave and covered the kitchen in baked beans. And no—not even I cover my baked beans with cling film when I'm microwaving them. Like Dad says, "Life is too short to give food an overcoat."

All this makes me giggle.

My laughing makes Lauren cross. "Seriously, though, Millie. LOOK at your exercise bike pic. Someone even said, 'This is everything. Give me more of your life hacks,' and LOOK at who liked that comment!"

I scroll through them again. Danny Trudeau thinks it's a good idea. The new boy has noticed me.

This is not a massive deal. How many random things do you like in a day? Bet you can't name them. I can't. Besides, I'm not about impressing men. I do silly stuff for me.

Lauren won't be stopped. "You could be a major Internet star. I've been thinking about it ALL night. You should do . . . something. I just can't think of what. . . ."

Dave jumps into Lauren's lap and lies on her back with her paws straight in the air. She truly does not care about anything or anyone. She does what she likes when she—

It's then that it hits me. I grab Dave. "CATS!"

Lauren starts shouting, "Yes! Let's make Dave a vlogging superstar! Cats always get likes."

"I'm not sure Dave will, though, Lozza. I don't think she understands vlogging. But let's have a go anyway?"

I get my phone out, look straight into the camera, and start recording.

"This is Dave, and I'm Millie. You see a lot of entertaining cats online. But Dave isn't like the cats you usually see."

At this point, Lauren catches on and pulls a bag of Doritos from her bag. She tries to balance a Dorito on Dave's nose. Dave just lies there with her legs still in the air. Lauren then piles up a cuddly llama (Aunty Teresa's), a science textbook (mine), and a chicken marengo sandwich (Lauren's—it looks vile) around Dave.

Dave still just lies there. I carry on.

"As you can see, if you want to make your cat go viral, get one that at least reacts to bread."

At that moment, Aunty Teresa bursts into my bedroom with her masses of black curly hair and her very neon spotty shirt. She's like a big cloud of slightly manic. She's also really loud. She takes one look at Lauren and Dave and shouts, "I'm sorry to barge in, Mills, but I heard what you've been talking about, and all I'm saying is: VEGETABLES!"

I pause the recording. I don't want to look completely stupid. Suddenly, you can see that what I've been saying about Aunty Teresa makes quite a lot of sense.

Lauren looks puzzled for about half a second, then she and Aunty

Teresa start jumping into the air, shouting, "VEGETABLES!! VEGETABLES!!!"

I sit there, zombielike.

"Haven't you seen it?!" Lauren is staring at me like I've suddenly grown four extra heads and an arm.

The worry rises in me like a tight anxiety burp. Usually "Haven't you seen it?!" means something involving you that everyone else knows about and you don't. I whisper, "Seen what?"

"MILLIE! Where have you been?!" Lauren says, getting her phone out. She shows me a cat jumping thirty feet into the air after being ambushed by a cucumber. Apparently this is a thing—this cat has had over five million views and four figures of likes.

A cucumber. Probably the most un-terrifying vegetable except for turnips, and they are pathetic AND unpopular.

Aunty Teresa dashes downstairs and brings back a real-life cucumber, three potatoes, a mandarin, and a cauliflower. We remove the sandwich from Dave, and for the next twenty minutes, we film Dave with vegetables.

This includes:

1. Lauren putting a cucumber by Dave. Dave cuddles it.
2. Aunty Teresa rolling potatoes in front of Dave. Dave ignores them.
3. Lauren giving Dave fake eyebrows with mandarin segments. This is quite funny.
4. Lauren making a small helmet for Dave from cauliflower leaves. Dave pulls them off in a really undramatic way.

Then I get a message that the storage is nearly full on my phone.

"*There you are! How NOT to make a cat vlog with me, Millie Porter, Lauren, and Aunty Teresa!*"

As I press STOP, MUM thunders into the bedroom like a really cross elephant in gym clothes, and Dave decides to rear up on two legs, leap six feet into the air, do a somersault, and land perfectly. The camera is OFF.

Lauren is very impressed. "Wow, Mrs. Porter, can you just do that again so I can turn the camera on and . . . get . . ."

You can tell by my mum's face that it really is time to totally shut up. Aunty Teresa has a rare moment of being a bit sensitive and grabs Lauren. "Anyway, do you want to go and increase our brain bandwidth with some more vlog ideas?"

Lauren says, "Er . . . yeah," and they disappear really quickly. It's just me, Mum, and Dave.

"Millie," Mum says, "I've brought some more of your stuff around. I thought you might want your school things sooner rather than later. And why have you got a piece of holly on your head?"

"I'm a Christmas pudding—it's cold," I snap. It's very difficult to be taken seriously when you are a dessert or a panda.

Mum shakes her head and leaves. She shouts, "I'm going to unload the car." I hear her muttering as she trips over something on the stairs. That would never happen at her house.

I should be using this time to go and help her, but I'm not. I'm going to keep my stupid hat on and edit and upload my new vlog. I think the bit with the cucumber was actually quite good. Family can wait a bit. It's vlog o'clock.

#GirlPower

Now, I have to admit, by the time Mum has carried all my stuff up to my room, I'm feeling a bit cross. I've only been here for one night and Mum is already checking up on me.

I bet I know why she's here. Mum reckoned I'd be ready to come home after one night. I used to hate sleepovers when I was little. So Mum thought I'd get panicky almost immediately and go back to her house in no time. Her plan has failed! I am stronger than she thinks!

I can tell that she is worried, though. She keeps walking around my new room, picking things up and putting them down again, opening and closing her mouth without a word. She looks like a music video on mute.

She tries to be nice. "Millie. If you're going to live here, you're going to have to make some little changes. They're ones that you deserve! The front door needs a proper lock. You need somewhere to hang your clothes and a desk for homework. And someone needs to remove that garden gnome that's doing you-know-what from the porch."

I know which one she means, but I say, "I haven't noticed it. What

I have noticed is how I can walk around this house without being attacked by a mop!"

"Well," Mum continues, "that's partly why I'm here. After you left last night, I had a chat with Gary. He has agreed to ONLY get McWhir—the robot vacuum cleaner—out every other day. So I want you to know that he is prepared to meet you halfway on the issue that maybe, *perhaps* he is over-cleaning."

"I'm not meeting anyone halfway!" I shout. Mum has ALWAYS told me that a strong woman doesn't give in. She fights for more. So I say, "Mum. I would like to see a complete cess . . . cess—"

Mum interrupts me and helps me with the word: *cessation*.

"Yes," I continue in, frankly, a very professional, almost-bossing-the-entire-situation way. "A complete cessation of the robot-hoover issue."

Mum looks sadly at me. "Well, Millie, that's not going to happen. Nor should it. Gary is trying. I'm trying. So should you. That's what ADULTS do."

The old Millie would have just shut up and done as she was told. But this is not old Millie. This is NEW Millie. Independent Millie. RESURGENT Millie (stole that from a film). RESURGENT MILLIE AHOY! And THIS Millie can fight back. . . .

"Well, MUM. I AM in a house full of adults, and THEY actually act like grown-ups rather than supercontrolling crazed people!"

At that moment, we both hear Dad shout from the kitchen, "Teresa! We cannot start using paper plates just because you don't want to spoil your Halloween nails by doing the washing-up. I don't care how long it took to do the vampire bat. Anyway, it's SEPTEMBER! It's TOO EARLY. Even for YOU!"

Mum only has to look at me and say, "You'll always have a room at my house, Millie. Come home."

It's scary and annoying. Mum can read me like a psychic. She can see that all this Dad-based chaos is actually quite hard to deal with.

Mum flounces out in a dazzle of Lycra. My mum rocks gym gear. She rocks everything.

She is totally magnificent and everything I would like to be. I can't tell her that, though. I'm too upset.

Downstairs, things have escalated. Teresa is claiming that you can scrub the bath by just having a bath when you are already clean and "rolling about a bit."

Wherever I live, cleaning causes problems.

I put some TV on and doze. It's all been a bit much. Too much emotional stuff makes me sleepy. Especially if I'm wearing a duvet.

When I wake up, I check my phone and squeal loud enough to make a dog deaf.

#Favorite

My cat vlog already has over a thousand views, which must be because it has been liked by the DAILY DANESH and he has COMMENTED!

> Great cat. Chill. Funny. Purrfect pet, YEAAHHHH.
> All the thumbs.

The Daily Danesh is one of the BEST vloggers around. He's a boy who lives with his grandma and created Frozen-Food Jenga. (He made a sixty-inch tower of frozen fish fingers and potato wedges!) He's a LEGEND, and HE HAS SEEN ME. He must like the fact that my female cat is called Dave.

It seems that Dave not being a viral sensation is actually quite funny. I can see in other places that the vlog's been shared by loads of people at school . . . including Danny Trudeau.

I think he's just trying to sort of be "in" with everyone.

You can stop thinking what I KNOW you're thinking. No. He does not fancy me. He doesn't even know me! This is real life—not

Disney. Boys like him don't fall into Big Hug Time with girls like me. You know what I mean.

I take a screengrab and change my bio to *Favorited by the Daily Danesh* because this is huge and just what I needed after my mum made me feel like I was about seven years old.

I run downstairs to tell everyone. Teresa and Dad are arm wrestling, so I tell Granddad instead. He's not very impressed. In fact, he's rude.

"So someone you've never met before—you have absolutely no idea what he's REALLY like—decided that you've said something a bit good and pressed some sort of thumb symbol thing, and that's a cause for celebration?!"

I leap in the air, clap, and shout, "YES!"

"I know you're a clever girl, Millie," Granddad mumbles, "but I'm not going to get excited every time something tiny like that happens. You'll get a big head, and there's nothing worse than that. Especially in a woman."

I don't really want to do that "old people don't get it" thing but OLD PEOPLE REALLY DON'T GET IT, do they? Besides, perhaps if Granddad had given more praise to his children, they wouldn't currently be practicing WWE–style wrestling on the front-room carpet—they're in their late thirties!

Also, "Especially in a woman"?! I decide to make it my responsibility while I am here to drag Granddad into this century with some epic feminism.

Slightly deflated, I go back upstairs to the room that is not really my room. I realize that I didn't even say good-bye to my actual best friend due to my family's nonstop drama. I message her.

> **Sorry for earlier, Loz. Will think of vlogs that aren't about Miss Mad Cat! See you tomoz. BTW Daily Danesh liked it!**

I don't want to show off, but I am chuffed and minted and all the joys.

Lauren replies almost immediately with two hundred emojis and:

> **Class, Mills. C-L-A-S-S!**

It's an okay response, but, between you and me, I'm a bit disappointed. This is my best friend, and the Daily Danesh is big, so I reply:

> **Are you okay?**

If I'm being honest with you, that really means: "That was a bit of a rubbish message. Why? Are you okay?"

My phone pings, like, IMMEDIATELY.

> **No. They are yelling again. It's horrible.**

INSTANT GUILT. Why am I getting excited about a favorite when Lauren basically lives in the equivalent of one of those really horrible places you see on television, where there's constant war?

I message back.

Stay out of it. Do like I do when it gets to be too much. Put your headphones on, do some coloring, and remember: I think you ARE THE BEST.

Lauren sends back loads of hearts. Send the love. Feel the love. It's what you have to do, isn't it?! That is just properly sensible.

Can I tell you what I've noticed? Not many adults are feeling the love. Lauren's parents argue pretty much 24/7 about everything. During the summer holidays, while Lauren and I watched *Harry Potter and the Deathly Hallows Part 2,* her mum and dad had a row about everything from Lauren's swimming lessons (she didn't want to go) to Lauren's gerbil (was it dead or just really tired?) that lasted the ENTIRE film. When a boy wizard can save the entire world in the same time that you have screamed about a dead mouse thing, you should probably realize that you have problems.

My problem is that I now can't stop checking the views on my vlog. Maybe now that Danny has seen me online, I can actually say hi to him in real life at school tomorrow?

Or maybe I'll just stay quiet and safe and UNDER THE RADAR in real life.

#ParentPlan

When I see Lauren at school the next day before homeroom, she looks tired. "They shouted till about two in the morning," she moans. She pulls the books out of her locker in the corridor like she hates everything. "Millie, it was pretty horrible. It was slightly funny, though, when I heard my dad say, 'The way you arrange the spice rack is madness!' It's very difficult dealing with people who are getting really angry about coriander and ground nutmeg."

Lauren smiles but seems like she's about to sob, too. It's times like this when your best friend needs a lift, so I change the subject.

"What about the next vlog?" I'm talking very quietly because I don't want anyone else to know just yet. "How about a 'How NOT to Be a Parent' vlog? You and I have got lots of personal experiences we could share."

Lauren does a little jump in the air. She brightens up pretty much immediately. "I LOVE IT, MILLS! The point is that it's a global, universal issue. Like gaming. And makeup. All the big vlogs are about the stuff that is worldwide and really matters. Like cats and really amazing cakes."

I decide to just come out with it: "We could talk about your parents!"

Now, I know this is touchy, so I quickly say, "But we could disguise ourselves."

Lauren stares at me intensely. "We could totally wear huge wigs."

"Hm. Maybe not." I don't tell her that's possibly the worst idea in the world. I just gently say, "But I think if we start off by talking about it from our own—"

Lauren interrupts, "Like if I talk about the argument last night. I mean, loads of parents probably argue about swimming, gerbils, and the precise placement of herbs in the spice rack."

I can sense that she is being sarcastic.

"Actually, they probably do, Lauren. I bet that argument has happened the world over. I bet that if we did a vlog about that, we'd . . ."

Suddenly, the atmosphere around us goes icy cold. A shadow appears. We've been spotted. Hunted. Cornered.

"Well, well, well! Look who it is! Millie Porter! We ARE causing a bit of a stir, aren't we?"

Abandon the plans. Put all defenses up. Erin Breeler is coming this way.

#Copycat

Erin Breeler is not what you need first thing on a Monday morning. She is officially the worst start to the week since I had tonsillitis at Christmas.

She glides up to both of us like she's on demon fairy wheels. Miranda, her fluffy best friend, is by her side. Erin towers over us, and we press our backs against our lockers. She is tanned and made-up brilliantly. Her lashes flutter like a flock of butterflies. Do butterflies come in flocks? They do on Erin's eyes. Seriously, if I didn't hate her so much, I'd be completely impressed. I try to keep calm, but inside, I feel the fear. My palms are sweating and leaving big print marks on my math book.

She purrs at us. And it's not a Dave-style purr. "All praise the Wardrobe Queen!" She laughs. "What a clever use of a piece of exercise equipment. I'm impressed, Millie. Really."

"Er . . . yeah," I say. This is RUBBISH. Why can't I think of something better? It's like that time Dad wrapped Aunty Teresa's head in Scotch tape. She couldn't say or do a thing. JUST LIKE ME NOW.

"I really did think it was good," Erin continues. "An unexpectedly funny, smart post."

I've still got mental tape all around my brain and body, so I just say, "Thank you."

"It was so good," Erin carries on, "that I thought it could do with a little bit of . . . improvement."

Suddenly, something in my head springs back into action.

"And what form would that 'improvement' take, Erin?" I sound a bit hard but not too ridiculous.

"It's no big deal, Millie. It's just about knowing what you're doing on Instagram. I mean, what you did was great, but you can't hope for too big a reach without . . . upping your game."

Now my tummy isn't full of Erin's butterflies. It's full of buffalo—galloping through fields, trampling everything in their path. My stomach is just a mass of HOOVES.

"And how is that?" I just about manage to get that out despite the total-body stampede.

Erin smirks her perfect smirk. She pulls out her phone, tosses it lightly in the air, and catches it perfectly. It's Cirque du Soleil with the latest Samsung. "Using good filters. Posting at the right time. Decent hashtags. The right audience for the content. That sort of thing. But it's okay, Millie, because I like to help if I can."

Feeling ever so slightly like I'm going to throw up, I ask her what she's done.

"Oh, don't let me tell you, Millie. Just go look. Look . . . and LEARN. Oh, and Lauren, I thought those heels were fab. It's just a shame how some people can't cope with real fashion, but I'm sure you'll get there eventually!" Then she flounces off down the hallway with Miranda, who just smirks and nods like a smirky, noddy thing.

I grab my phone and go straight to Erin's account. When I see what she's done, I want to go off like Gary when he's spotted pink mold in the shower.

Erin "TOTAL EVIL" Breeler has reposted my photo to her account and given it a different—and YES, much better—filter, and it got hundreds of likes in under an hour. What's even worse? She captioned it:

> Don't fancy working out? Don't worry, girls, here's
> a great hack from @MilliePorter. If you're not a
> #GymBunny, you can always use your gear as
> a wardrobe instead. Remember: If you want to make
> high-street fashion last, take care of your clothes. ;)
> #Glow #BudgetFashion #LifeHacks

Erin looks back at me from down the hall and sees that I have seen her evil. "It's a great message, Millie," she shouts. "I like helping people. You're helping them, too. We did it together. It's like . . ." And she pauses and does that face of MAXIMUM MINX. "It's like you and I, for that tiny minute, were a team."

Then she walks off. She's a trap, and I just stepped right into her.

We can't speak. We don't say anything for about three hours. It might be less than that, but it feels that long. Lauren just stares at me and finally says, "How does she manage to always be . . . right?"

I sigh. "She's clever. This is a whole new world of terrible, Lauren. Even when you do good stuff, she finds a way to make you feel terrible about it. Now all her followers will think I'm a complete idiot and troll me to death."

"What do you think we should do?" At times like this, Lauren assumes I have the answer, and usually I do. But not this time.

"Well, there's nothing that we can do—we've just got to take it and . . ."

"And?" Lauren puts her arm around me.

"I need to think," I say.

Actually, I need to think for a very long time.

#ZenLoo

At lunchtime, I find my quiet, secret place. I need it sometimes. No. I can't tell you. It's secret.

Okay. Farthest cubicle to the right in the loo nearest the science classrooms. Trust me, it's Zen Central.

Most people have no idea what power words have these days. Mum told me once that a group of girls used to stand at the end of her street and call her names. There were six of them. She told me that story like she was majorly traumatized. Six people on one street in one town. That's IT! That's all.

How can I explain to her that now there can be thousands and millions of people laughing at you within a minute of you doing something stupid? Or NOT even that stupid? The sort of people who follow Erin are going to be laughing at me, thinking I'm tragic.

I take some deep breaths. Sometimes it's best not to think about things too much.

I don't fire back and do something rash, because that's not my style. You've got to plan, and I'm a thinker.

First, I'm going to think about my breathing. Normally, my lungs work just fine by themselves, but now I start noticing that my chest is going up and down and my body seems like it's getting smaller. It happens every time I'm really worried. And I can keep it together by just being on my own for a few minutes. Nipping off to the Zen Loo is always a very good idea.

I come out. Lauren's waiting for me outside. She's used to this. She doesn't say anything, but she knows.

I'm calm.

Or I am until I spot Danny Trudeau and his incredible vintage orange rucksack. He is heading my way, looking like a sexy tangerine, and my BFF is frantically digging me in the ribs. Happening now: panic.

"Hi, Millie!" Danny bounds over to me like we're old friends. We aren't. I wish we were. "I just want to say I absolutely loved your vlog with Dave the cat. Someone mentioned it in art this morning, and I was . . . it was FUNNY. I'm a cat freak, though. I love them. I had to leave mine behind in Canada with my uncle. His name is Benny. I Skype him, but cats aren't great at the talking thing. A bit like the way Dave isn't that great at attacking vegetables. Anyway, your vlog was . . . really good."

I don't really know what to say. I'm not hugely good at the whole compliment thing. But I don't want to be giggly and stupid near men, so I try to change the subject. I jog around my head, trying to think of something funny and witty and magnificent to say. Something that will make this boy think I'm cool and smart and generally . . .

"You've got a great-looking lunch there!"

You've. Got. A. Great-looking. Lunch. There.

But no, my brain hasn't stopped. It wants to say more. . . .

"Good container, too. Sturdy!"

Dear Sensible Millie's Mind: Thanks for nothing. Good-bye.

Danny Trudeau looks at me like I've said something really random. This is because I *have* said something really random. Eventually, he replies with: "Yeah! Chinese mum. French dad. The world's best food all in one box."

"À la noodles!" my head blurts out. If Danny thought I was funny before, my brain has convinced him that I am actually not.

Danny smiles a bit and looks down. There's a pause and then he says, "Well . . . I'd better be going to . . . finish this. Bye, Millie. Hello—is it Lauren? You were in that vlog, too! Bye, Lauren!"

Lauren manages to wave. My brain hasn't recovered from the *À la noodles!* comment and can't form a sentence.

Danny Trudeau and his gourmet lunch drift off like steam. I collapse on a bench. Lauren drops beside me with her jaw on the floor.

"What happened there?!" Lauren isn't used to seeing me so utterly useless. "You were . . . oh, Millie! You really like him, don't you?!"

I groan.

Lauren puts her arm around me. "Don't worry! Perhaps he likes talking about . . . kitchen storage—"

In the middle of saying it, Lauren realizes she sounds ridiculous and tries something else. "He thinks you're really funny!"

I have a bad feeling that Danny Trudeau and lots of other people are laughing AT me, not WITH me. I really need to get away from school as soon as I can.

#DadRescue

When I get home, I find that Dad has taken all the cuddly toys from my bedroom and the exercise bike is now in the hall. Apparently, Mum gave him strict orders to make a lovely room for me. Yes! But I feel a bit bad. The bike is now a place to put coats, junk mail, charity collection bags, and the red bills that my dad seems to get all the time. It will never be something to increase your actual fitness on.

Granddad corners me when I go downstairs to make a cup of tea.

"You look fed up, love. Everything okay?"

I tell him nearly everything. I can see him looking puzzled. Finally, he blurts out, "I don't get it. Why are you bothered by the opinions of people you've never met in your life, orchestrated by some person who needs taking down a peg or two? Just ignore her!"

But I can tell that he's worried, because I hear him go straight into the front room and tell Dad that I'm being that "new style of modernly bullied."

Dad comes straight upstairs, hugs me, and says, "Mills, do you want me to go up to the school and sort this out?"

I show him the photo. "Here's the problem: I posted the photo. I shared it first. She just shared it again and credited me like she should have done, but she basically said that I'm tragic. She's done nothing wrong. Really. Well, she has, but she's . . . Dad, she is EXTREMELY clever. You can't beat her."

Dad stares at me intensely and says, "You're right, Millie. Keep away from her. She's clearly a bit of a genius. Focus on your friends. You're still friends with Lauren, aren't you?"

That isn't really what I wanted to hear. I wanted more than that. God, I miss Mum. She'd know what to do. Dad tries, but he just hasn't got Mum's amazing wisdom. It makes this whole house seem a bit . . . wobbly.

Dad goes back downstairs. Despite my frankly enormous and clever brain YELLING, *Don't read the comments, Millie!*, I can't help myself. I look at Erin's account again. The likes have gone up to over a thousand, and the comments are *horrible*:

Who would live like that? Selfish to the earth

Awful jeans! No point taking care of those LOL

SLOTH! :-)

Great advice E

Wow, that room could do with a decent tidy and a paint job.

Now, I know I've been moaning a bit about my room, but Dad *is* trying and Granddad is old! He doesn't care about repainting.

> **This person needs to get some respect for themselves and their clothes.**

Just as I can feel my chest getting tight again, I see another comment:

> **Erin—you are just evil for doing this. Stop being so fake.**

It's from @misslaurenmeister—Lauren's account. She's brave and loyal and lovely . . . and very, very stupid.

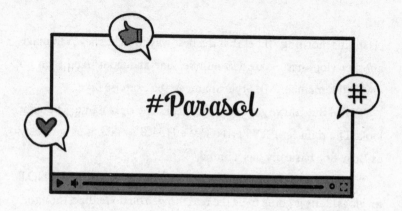

#Parasol

I call Lauren immediately. Every second that comment is on there, someone could see it and report back. And when Erin sees it or hears about it, she isn't going to be happy that someone has accused her of being less than perfect in front of her followers. She will take things even more nuclear. She'll use Weapons of Mass Social Media Destruction.

Lauren picks up the phone after no rings. "I know, I know," she yelps, "but I just can't take that girl any longer. We have to stand up to her, Millie. We have to stick our heads above the parasol!"

"*Parapet.*" I have to correct her.

"Yeah, whatever—what is a parapet?"

I google it. "It's 'a low, protective wall along the edge of a roof, bridge, or balcony.'"

"Yes!" Lauren shouts. "We need to stick our entire bodies over the social-media parapet and put up an anti–Erin parasol to guard against her onslaught of being . . . fantastic. I will delete the comment, though. Hopefully she's waxing and hasn't seen!"

I tell Lauren my plan. I've been thinking about it since the hallway clash this morning. "I bet that the best way to fight back is to make another vlog that makes US number one at school. And then no one will remember Mr. Style Shame *or* the exercise bike."

"YES! But you've got to do it RIGHT. The right name. The right look. The right EVERYTHING. We HAVE to take it as seriously as Erin. She basically has a brand."

"You're right, Lauren. No more cats or pandas or 'How NOT to' vlogs. This is going to be the real thing. You do realize, though," I say, "that this means she *will* go for us, Loz? It's not just sticking our heads above the parasol."

"*Parapet!* Now you're getting it wrong!" Lauren giggles.

This makes me laugh, too. "Yes. That. Again. This is us sticking our heads above the entire world and saying, 'ERIN BREELER! We are here with our vlog, and it's about the things that REALLY matter. It's the stuff-that-really-matters vlog!' I know! How about we talk about how we deal with school, home, boys, makeup—we can cover everything?! EVERYTHING THAT MATTERS EVER AND EVERYTHING THAT WILL EVER MATTER! And we can start with . . ."

I trail off. I sound ridiculous.

"Yeah. This might need a bit of thought, Mills." Lauren sounds uncomfortable. "And what should we call it? If we're taking on Erin, we can't sound like spoons."

She's right.

Lauren pauses and whispers, "Perhaps we can make up a really smart pseudo–cyber bully called Tarryn Teeler?!"

"Oh, Lozza, I'm not sure that will work. I know—I'll come over after school tomorrow, and we can discuss and plan fully."

I get off the phone and trip over a tennis ball that has rolled out from under the bed. Our next vlog will have to be filmed somewhere quiet, where there is little chance of someone crazy coming in, and when I hear Teresa singing about her latest Tinder date, I know that means *not here*.

#OnLocation

"Well, we can't film it here, Mills. Listen!"

When we get back to Lauren's house, her parents are not shouting. It's silent. And immaculately tidy. Perfect conditions for vlogging, in fact.

"Why can't we?" I ask.

"Because it's always really quiet before they start up again."

This annoys me a bit. I was counting on Lauren's house. I know her parents are rubbish, but I'm not in a great domestic situation, either! Surely we can make a vlog without them getting in the way. I try to persuade her. . . .

"But we can't do it at my granddad's. It's chaos, and no one understands privacy. Aunty Teresa comes into my bedroom every other minute."

Lauren bows her head. "Millie. We can't do it here."

"Are you sure?" The vlog is such a good idea. I don't want to let it go AND I want to get it just right.

"Millie. There is a soccer match on tonight. Mum wants to watch it. Dad doesn't. That makes Dad rant about old girlfriends and the way Mum still wears floral dresses and Doc Martens even though she's forty-one."

This outrages me! "But they look cool! That's totally ageist!"

"I know," Lauren sighs. "He's just cross. He doesn't really mean it."

This makes me think. "We should do a vlog on discrimination, too, Loz. There are loads of things to cover. Feminism. Sexism. Should you wear makeup when you're campaigning for a better, fairer world? Or something."

"Whatever, Millie—we can't do it here. Seriously."

I have another major-breaking-news brain flash of excellence. "I know where we can do it. We will have to time it just right, though. . . . My mum's house. I don't want to go back there, but my room would be perfect!"

Lauren looks horrified. "But you're not living there anymore!"

"I know!" I wink. "But I've still got my key."

"What about the Neat Freak?" Lauren asks.

"He works late on Wednesdays and Thursdays. If we time it right with his shift and Mum's, we'll be fine! Tomorrow after school. We'll have exactly forty-five minutes. We can DO THIS! TRUST!"

This is me pulling out my credit card of good ideas. It never lets me down.

#Burglars

We go straight from school to my mum's. It's deathly quiet. We creep up to my old bedroom and open the door. It's Wednesday, and Gary's away. The normal world can play!

When I get inside, I can see that someone has already dusted the blinds, even to the far-corner bits. No one does that. I bet even Prince Harry's blinds are filthy bad there. It's cleaner than it has been in a very long time. And it was only a little dirty in the first place. I am fully aware of the many diseases that come from dust and bed mites. I've seen those photos of bed bugs that have been magnified to a million times their actual size. When I can't sleep, I often google illnesses. It's good to know what could kill you.

"Right," Lauren says. "First things first. What's our vlog going to be about?"

I flip out some notes I've scribbled down. Mum always says that preparation stops poor performance.

WHY can't I get Mum out of my head?

"EPIC!" Lauren shouts. "Now we need to prepare THE FACES."

Lauren's makeup collection is extensive. Her mum and dad buy her something every time they feel guilty about shouting and upsetting her. Which is a lot.

We spend serious time getting the base right, and then we thoroughly contour for the screen. We go high gloss on the lips and dark on the eyes.

Lauren looks at us both. "Yes. The effect is professional but approachable. It says we mean business but you can also talk to us on a level that you're comfortable with. It's the look of today's pressured, professional woman. *We work. We nurture. We deliver.*"

I try not to laugh, but I do. "Loz, you spoon, where did you get that from?"

Lauren laughs, too. "I saw it on *This Morning* when I was home sick with conjunctivitis. Seriously. It's 'makeup with a message.'"

We both end up giggling. "Loz, we need to be quiet. If Mum finds out we were here, she'll think that I can't cope at Granddad's."

"Well, you can't." Lauren is all sheepish and apologetic. "You're Miss Particular and that house feels like a party popper has just gone off ALL THE TIME."

I do a death stare. "No, it's just not right for vlogging. That's different."

Lauren can see that I'm a bit miffed so she takes some fairy lights off my mirror and dangles them in the air above my head.

"Shall I hold the lights like this behind you?"

I do not want my best friend standing behind me like a Christmas tree. It will make us look like those wacky joke vloggers. That's not what we're about. I'm not saying we can't be funny, but we also have really serious stuff to discuss.

"Loz, I want you sitting with me. Okay—how should we start? I've been thinking our first subject should be—"

Lauren interrupts me. "Well, I thought we could just say who we are . . . and then totally wing it. Be natural. Talk from the heart!" And then Lauren just stares at me.

I try not to get cross. I do think we need to be a little more prepared than that, but I don't want to be too bossy and Miss Know-It-All to Lauren. That's old Millie. Mum-influenced Millie. I'm trying to live more in the moment now, so I say, "Yeah! Let's go for it."

I press RECORD on my phone, and we both say, "*Hello!*" then collapse into giggles.

"It's okay! We can edit it!" I say. "Take two. Take two."

"Take two what?!" Lauren looks very confused.

"That's what directors say," I explain. "TAKE two! Okay. This one. Really this one."

We turn the camera on and giggle again.

"Lauren!" I yell.

"I'm sorry." She snorts through laughs. "It's just, you know . . . too . . . you know!"

"I know." I get it. "Right. Let's think of something really serious."

Lauren stares at me and says, "Death."

And we still can't stop laughing.

"What is wrong with us?!" I ask. "Are we terrible people?! We are laughing at death!"

And then Lauren collapses on my fluffy rug, shaking with the giggles.

"It's not even funny," I yell, but I can't stop laughing, either.

Then suddenly, I hear a noise outside the door. "Lauren. Shhhhh! I think Mum's back! Or Gary!"

Someone is coming down the landing toward my bedroom. We've been making so much noise, they must think we're really rubbish burglars. My heart starts to pound. I can see Lauren looking at me for comfort, but I can't give her any. I'm scared, too.

She whispers, "What if they bash us over the head with something or call the police? Or call the police, THEN bash us over the head?!"

"Shhhh!" I snap. "It's going to be okay." I don't believe this for one moment.

The door creaks open slightly. Someone is checking to see who the intruders are. Unless . . . My brain starts an insane worry spiral. What if burglars are actually disturbing *us*? What if some prisoners have escaped and they want a really tidy safe house with a good selection of soups and non-crumbly biscuits? We are in trouble. I can sense it. I know it. This is bad. This is serious. . . .

This is—

McWhirter, the robot vacuum cleaner, glides into the room on full spin and starts trying to hoover up Lauren, who is still on the floor. He must be preprogrammed to start cleaning automatically. He has a little base at the top of the staircase that he sits in when he's doing the upstairs.

I scream very angrily, "McWhirter!"

"Don't upset him." Lauren bites her lip. "Perhaps he'll tell Gary or something!"

"How can he, Lauren?! He's a robot!"

Lauren narrows her eyes. "Perhaps he has a surveillance device on him. Perhaps a tiny camera is relaying all this to your mum via satellite right now. Perhaps she doesn't really work at a hospital. Perhaps she's employed by the government to spy on teenagers everywhere, and robot vacuums are actually just cameras that clean!"

It's then that I decide we need to get out of here.

"Lauren, we are catching the weird off this house. This is why I wanted to go to Granddad's in the first place. Let's get out of here."

"What about the vlog?" Lauren looks GUTTED. This is her big dream, too.

"We just need another plan. We're not giving up. Let's go back to my granddad's, get some dinner, and have a think." I put my arm around her.

I haven't got a clue where we can film, but Lauren doesn't need to know that right now.

#ShedOfSense

When we get back to Dad's house, he and Teresa are
having a karaoke session. Teresa is in the middle of a serious power
ballad. Dad is howling like a dog in pain. They have loads of fun
together, but no one has done the important jobs. A sheet of lint
has collected in the back of the dryer. The house is Mess HQ, and
it's why everything is on the brink of catching fire.

The safest thing is to go out and see Granddad. As usual, he's in
his shed. He spends a lot of time there. He may not understand
women or the Internet, but perhaps he has some idea of a place to
film that is slightly sane and quiet.

I knock on the shed door. Lauren waits outside; the shed can fit
two but not three. Granddad is sitting there asking a tiny rose in a
tiny pot why "she" refuses to bud. Though this sounds a bit weird,
it's easier to deal with than what is happening indoors.

"Granddad, can you . . . ?"

All of a sudden, I have an odd thought.

Granddad's shed would be a perfect vlogging space if we just
moved all the gardening equipment, the potted plants, the green

netting, his tools and pieces of wood, and his calendar featuring Britain's favorite seashore-wading birds.

Granddad spots me eyeing it up. "I imagine that you want to come in here for some reason. Quiet. Nice big inside lock that keeps the whole world out. . . . I may let you use this shed, but don't you be taking my bar-tailed godwit, Millie. I want that calendar kept up there."

Granddad is slightly psychic.

"I was just wondering if Lauren and I could use your shed for a bit of filming. We want to make a vlog," I say.

Granddad peers at me with his detective-inspector-investigating-a-murder face. "What's a vlog? Is it illegal?"

"No, Granddad! It's, like, a video that you can upload to a site and then everyone can watch it!"

"But why would people want to watch it?"

Granddad doesn't mean to be harsh. He just really does not get it.

"Because," I explain, "you've got something to tell people that might help them or make them laugh or—"

"So what are you going to tell them? What can YOU do?"

Okay. He IS sounding harsh now. And Captain Sexist of HMS *Patronizing*.

When I answer him, I sound a bit sharp. "I'm starting a funny advice vlog. On how to deal with life and idiots and families and trolls."

Granddad stares at me. "You do know trolls aren't real, don't you, Millie? I mean, I know we told you that they lived under bridges and frightened the Three Billy Goats Gruff, but they—"

I do lose my patience slightly here. "Granddad. A *troll* is someone who keeps hassling you on social media and the Internet." I try to make it simple. Lauren nods behind me.

"Well, just tell them to stop it," Granddad says.

I'm trying to be patient. I REALLY am. "It doesn't work like that. You can tell them to stop it, but they just carry on."

Granddad's face reddens and his fists clench. He shouts, "Tell a teacher then! Or me! I could sort them out for you, love."

This melts me a bit, but I don't know where to start.

"The thing is, you don't always know who they are, Granddad." I'm thinking of Mr. Style Shame. "Or you can't prove that they're really being horrible." Now I'm thinking of Erin Breeler.

Granddad studies me. "Millie. I don't know if I want you being in that world much."

"That world? It is *the* world!" I yell.

"Well, young ladies have to look after themselves."

Granddad has a thing about young ladies having to be careful. It makes me cross.

"So do young gentlemen," I snap. "Please, can I use this shed?"

"You can use it, Millie. Because you're not a daft girl. Your dad's crackers gene missed you. But . . . just be careful. Look after yourself, then look after everyone else."

Granddad always says this to me. It seems a bit selfish to me, but *he* is selfish. He had all his laundry done and dinner made for him for thirty-five years. He doesn't really understand thinking about others.

But he's helping me, so I just give him a hug and say, "Thank you."

Granddad nods. As he leaves the shed, he says, "By the way, I'll sort the tumble dryer before the whole place goes up."

Granddad is like me. He likes me. He gets me. I love him.

I call Lauren in. "Granddad says we can use his shed for the vlog!"

Lauren says, "You sure, Mills? It's not very glam."

I explain that we don't have an alternative and that we are NOT allowed to touch the bird calendar.

Lauren is disgusted. "We can't do a serious vlog with a bird in the background."

I can see her point. "Let's change it to a different month," I suggest. "Perhaps there will be a better bird."

Lauren flips through the common sandpiper, the curlew, and the whimbrel before she asks me whether the Temminck's tragopan looks "a bit sexy with its incredible Olympic cyclist legs."

I give her a bit of a look. "It's a bird!" My best friend's gone off the planet. I need to get her back. "Leave it on the bar-tailed godwit," I tell her. "Let's get started. Granddad's not going to let us stay in here forever."

Lauren pulls her superserious face. There's a long pause before she murmurs, "You know . . . well . . . I honestly think you should do it on your own."

"What?!" The whole point was that this is something good that Lauren and I can do TOGETHER.

"Mills, all I'll end up doing is repeating what you say AND interrupting you! I will sound STUPID. I didn't even want to do it that much at your mum's. Seriously. I thought I would want to, but I don't."

"Lauren, I'm gutted. Please do it with me!" I'm begging a bit now, but I don't care. "You're funny, and people love you. You don't even have to try! And you look amazing!"

Lauren's eyes are on the floor.

"No. You do it on your own, but I want to direct, do your makeup, dress the set, and perhaps be off-camera."

And then Lauren admits the real reason why she doesn't want to be on-screen. "I just hate how I look even WITH the contouring. I looked like such a spoon on Mr. Style Shame. I hate my legs. And when I speak on camera, I get twenty-five chins!"

This makes me really angry. "Everyone has twenty-five chins, Lauren! If you didn't have all those, your neck would split and your head would fall off."

Perhaps we should vlog about that—people who don't want to be on film because they hate the way they look, even when they are totally wrong about it.

"I don't want to talk about it, Mills," Lauren snaps.

I get it.

"Have you been trolled? Lauren! Don't let them get to you! Turn them off!"

This is great advice, but I don't know if I would follow it.

Lauren gets angry. "Millie, I don't want to talk about it, but I can help with the other things. If I'm going to direct and dress the set, then I'm going to tell you what I really think: Before you do your first vlog, you could do with some expert advice so it looks good. I don't mean YOU looking good—I mean IT looking good. We are in a shed. We need all the help we can get. Who do we know that does great videos or stuff online?"

"Erin Breeler and loads of famous people who won't help us."
Yes. I'm getting breathless again now. This was exciting. Now it's
going bad very quickly.

"We do know someone who can help," Lauren says sort of sheep-
ishly. "Bradley Sanderson."

"Bradley Sanderson? The king of lifts and escalators?! But we're
not going to be vlogging about machines."

"It doesn't matter what he vlogs about, Millie. The point is that
he does it really well. He gets loads of views! You should ask him
about it at school tomorrow. And keep out of Erin's way."

Erin. She'd make my advice vlog into something about bird-
watching and wading birds in an instant. I can't imagine her EVER
posting anything filmed in a potting shed. Lauren is totally right. I
need James Bond's geek genius, the one who sorts out his gadgets.
I need Bradley Sanderson to be my secret weapon.

#GeekHelp

Finding Bradley Sanderson is not as simple as I thought.
I try on Thursday at lunchtime. We're not supposed to use our phones during school hours, so I suspect he's hiding in the shadows somewhere. It can't be easy to have a hugely successful but absolutely terminally dorky vlog. Your friends must be mainly online, not offline.

I try the library, the computer lab, the empty ninth-grade classrooms, and just about every corner that exists in the school. Eventually, I lift up a massive, furry parka in the lost and found closet. Bradley is hidden underneath. With just the light of his phone in his eyes, he looks really spooky. He has thick-rimmed, geek-chic glasses and a floppy fringe. His hair is like a blind he can pull across his face.

"What do you want?" Bradley peers up at me.

"Hello, Bradley. I'm Millie Porter from seventh grade. I was wondering if you could help me with my vlog?" I'm feeling a bit nervous about talking to him.

"Ah! A damsel in distress. 'Help me, Obi-Wan!' she says. 'You're my only hope.' I don't think we've met before, but now, because it's about vlogging, you want my help!"

I think Bradley is being a bit snarky. Maybe I'm not the first person to try to make friends with him for social-media advice. I'm clearly out of my depth, but I want to learn. So I carry on.

"Well, you're a bit like a famous bat—we all know about you, but no one sees you in daylight. You have loads of subscribers, Bradley. Please, will you let me know your secret?"

This seems to soften Bradley a bit. "What's your vlog about?"

I sit beside him underneath a blazer. It feels weird but right at the same time. I try to explain. "Well, I want to make a vlog that will help people. People who don't always fit in at school or are finding it hard at home or who are being trolled. But it's not going to be all Captain Dullard advice. It will be silly, too!"

Bradley glances down at his phone. I get the sense that this might not be the greatest idea for a vlog he's ever heard. "Vlogs are easy. Do it in landscape on your phone. Download an app. The app talks to your laptop. Upload and edit."

Bradley clearly thinks I am very stupid indeed. Talk about mansplaining.

"I know all that. I mean, how do you get people really interested? How do you get people to subscribe? What's the right way to talk to your subscribers?"

Bradley looks up again and smiles. "Millie, I'm happy to give you advice. But it isn't as simple as having the right hashtags or uploading stuff regularly."

"But, Bradley, I really, really need some help! I've never done this before. All I've got is my granddad's shed and a best friend who's great at contouring! And a cat!"

I'm feeling pretty desperate, and it's starting to get rather hot under this blazer. "Look, I'm not being funny, but can we come out from under these blazers, and I'll—"

Suddenly, the coats lift up and I see something that takes every single bit of oxygen away from my body, even though that isn't actually possible or I would die.

It's Danny Trudeau. Looking at us.

I lose control of some of my atoms and my brain blurts out the first thing it can think of. "We are not kissing!" I bark, pointing at Bradley.

Bradley agrees so quickly that it's almost a bit rude. "No. We are NOT."

"Hello, Millie! And don't worry, it's none of my business." Danny beams. His smile is like the northern lights. Probably. It's certainly like a really beautiful screen saver featuring the sky at night with all the stars. "It's just—that's my blazer." He gestures to the coat I've currently got draped over my sweating forehead.

As I try to untangle myself, going EVEN redder in the process, I manage to blurt out some words: "We're just talking about vlogging!"

Danny leans on the wall and winks. "Of course you were. Sorry to disturb you!"

I don't want him to go, so I keep talking. "Yeah, so I'm thinking of doing an advice vlog. Sort of following on from the other stuff I've done with the bike, the panda, and Dave."

This sounds ridiculous when I say it out loud.

"Who's Dave?" asks Bradley.

Danny purses his lips together. "Yeah . . . That sounds . . ." When he thinks, he gets a crease in his forehead. "Yeah!" Suddenly, he brightens. "I know! You could call it something short and quick and memorable, like . . . HASHTAG Help!"

I leap up. "Hashtag Help! Danny, that's actually fantastic. Thank you!"

"It was your idea," Danny says. "I was just your muse."

I have no idea what Danny means, so I just say, "Yes!"

"Anyway!" Danny exclaims. "I've got to go. Enjoy your brainstorm." Then he drifts off like he's being carried by wings. And not the wings of a wading bird—the wings of a mighty, hot eagle.

When I regain a sort of sensible consciousness, Bradley is giving me a funny look. It's almost like he feels sorry for me. "Now THAT conversation, Millie Porter from seventh grade, would have made a great vlog!"

I regain some dignity. A bit.

"I was just slightly shocked at . . . that, but I need your help. I don't want to beg. I've got a name for it now at least! Will you please help me do something actually, possibly useful?"

Bradley sighs. "Come to the shopping center on Saturday. They've had Schindler MRL traction scenic elevators installed. Believe me, they are world class. I've had requests to film them."

"You've had people asking to see them?!" I find this very surprising.

"Yes, Millie. My vlog has global reach. Meet me there on Saturday at two o'clock. I'll try to help you a bit."

"It's a date!" I quickly correct myself. "Well, it's not a date, but you know what I mean. It's a date."

"Don't worry, Millie. I've got a girlfriend. She likes lifts, too. This isn't a date."

"I never knew you had a girlfriend! What grade is she in?" This is turning into a day of quite enormous surprises.

Bradley puffs up his chest and says in a rather cocky way, "She lives in the States. She's mainly into moving sidewalks and scenic escalators. That's how we met—online. I want to fly over to see her next year, but my mum doesn't really get it."

"They never get it. My mum is lovely, but she'd freak out if she knew I was thinking about vlogging."

Bradley raises one eyebrow. "She'll find out, Millie. They always do. If you have any success, she'll find out. See you Saturday. Got to go. Double math classes. Some relief from the hell that is this place." Bradley disappears, sort of clinging to the wall in a way that makes him invisible to other people.

Really, I should get to class. Really, I should tell Mum what I'm doing. Really, I should do a lot of things, but I'm too busy thinking about the fact that Danny saw me when I was pretending to be a pile of coats.

I am turning into a boy-crazy idiot. I need to stop. I hate it when girls go like that—dumping their friends for men and being ridiculous. And, besides, we all know what's going to happen to Danny Trudeau.

#Predictable

"He is totally going to end up going out with Erin Breeler."

During the Thursday afternoon torture that is Shakespeare, Lauren manages to say what the whole of our year is thinking. And it's a real tragedy.

"I know," I whisper. "I spoke to him at lunch and thought exactly the same thing. He even SMELLS good, like a really expensive oil diffuser."

Lauren giggles. "Expensive oil diffuser?! Like Gary has in his car? Christmas spruce and gingerbread? But how have you been close enough to him to smell him?"

How to explain this one? "I was under the coats with Bradley Sanderson, and he disturbed us."

Lauren looks like she has developed Seriously Miffed Disease and hisses, "I think your next vlog should be about when you don't tell your best friend about the biggest things that are happening in your life right now."

I have to spend the next five minutes reassuring Lauren that we were just having an undercover vlogging master class, which was her idea in the first place. When I finally convince her that she'll be the first to know WHENEVER I kiss someone, she shouts, "Now TELL ME what you found out about Danny!"

The class goes quiet. Erin Breeler and Miranda turn around and stare at us. Once we've been told to calm down by Mrs. Foss and are safely holding our copies of *Romeo and Juliet* in front of our faces, I have to admit that I don't know a lot more than she does. But I do tell her that he had the idea for #Help.

Lauren grunts. "There's a photo of him on Instagram. Well, of his back. Have you seen it?"

We hide my phone in my pencil case and find the photo. It's on Leanne Pilton's Instagram, which is mainly full of her dog. She managed to basically pat the back of the lovely Canadian. He looks Big Ben–tall and has a fantastic bum even in regulation school trousers.

"Should we be looking at a photo of a bum?" I ask Lauren. "I feel a bit wrong and sweaty. As feminists, we go after boys who do that to girls."

We stop looking. It's hard, but as Mum says, principles are often hard to carry, but that doesn't mean you should drop them. I keep the image in the guilty bit of my mind, though.

I know Lauren is still thinking about it, too. She starts off discussing the latest Mr. Style Shame post, but midway through talking about what everyone is now calling "the Pug Print Disaster," she changes the subject.

"You should share that you've spoken to Danny and that you like him, Millie. You're basically being a journalist by doing that. It's the breaking news everyone wants to know. OR you could just comment on Leanne's photo and say something like, 'Canada's a great place and full of quite excellent people' and then just add loads of winky faces and hearts. We'll know what you mean!"

The truth is, I do like him—even more so after the coat incident. It's not just his looks—it's his whole vibe. And why shouldn't I tell people I met him and he was nice?! I'm going to do JUST as Lauren says. That's what a strong woman does. I can't worry about what other people think ALL the time. I can't worry about what Erin might do or even if Danny might see it. That's sensible. I am sensible. IT IS SENSIBLE TO LIKE CANADA and share that fact. I have decided.

#TwoFaced

When I check my phone between classes, I find that the High Commission of Canada in the United Kingdom and someone called Annabelle D'Sa have favorited my comment. I suppose it doesn't really matter that actually the entire country of Canada thinks I love it.

Lauren agrees. "They are probably nice people, too. Their flag has a leaf on it that looks really approachable and friendly."

How can a leaf look friendly?

Lauren googles it. "Look at it! It's sort of jumping in the air and saying, 'Come in . . . to my hot tree!'"

"You're off your tree, Lauren—that's the basic problem."

We collapse into giggles.

"Seriously, though, Mills, we mustn't get distracted from the vlog. Let's see how things are going with the Dave one. Maybe someone's got an idea for Hashtag Help." Lauren flicks the phone out from her pocket.

The numbers haven't changed from last time. Not one more like. Not one more view.

I'm a bit gutted by this. However much #Help means to us, it's probably not going to be a success. How do people even become popular?! How do you win against all the celebrities, people jumping into frozen swimming pools, and experiments involving sticky goo and massive water balloons?! Or the Erin Breelers of this world?

Lauren sees that I'm down. "You know what you've got to do: When you see Bradley Sanderson on Saturday, you HAVE to get him to tell you how he gets so many hits for his stuff about boring stairs. Then we can start vlogging properly."

I will, but after today, I'm not sure he's going to tell me that much. I think he's probably just being kind. He's only really interested in his own thing, though. Between you and me, I admire him.

Anyway, I should just get over myself and ask for more advice.

"Yeah. You should . . . ask . . . or talk or . . . whatever you think is the right thing, Mills." Lauren seems distracted. "Sorry!" She sounds embarrassed. "I'm looking at the Instagram photo of the Canadian bottom again."

I'm still a bit uncomfortable with it. I would hate it if someone did that to me, but I just have a quick look. It is fabulous. It's a really tremendous view of someone's back. Since I commented on it, it's got loads of likes and more comments, including—

"Lauren. LOOK at the comments!" We're late for history now, but I am FULL of rage. We read it together.

I hope @LeanneP asked permission from
@DannyTruds before posting this #Creepy

It's from Erin.

She's also replied to my comment about Canada with the embarrassed monkey emoji. Maybe my Danny love wasn't so subtle after all.

Lauren points to the phone and says every word in slow motion. "Can you EVEN believe the total hypocrite, two-facedness of it? After what she did to you with the exercise bike . . . She really is a major piece of work."

I know the real reason why Erin is acting like Miss Moral Social Media. Hot boys unofficially belong to her till she says otherwise. And she has to be the first to know all the gossip. Still, we've been warned. . . . I explain this to Lauren, and she looks really impressed.

"You are basically a psychologist, Millie," she says. "You just need to do a vlog that's actually good and doesn't make you sound like a seven-year-old that's just got hold of his mum's phone while she's hanging out the washing."

I death-stare Lauren.

"It's a compliment. Sort of," she says.

#FakeFeminism

I am not wise. I'm certainly not brave. If I like Danny, I shouldn't let Erin stop me from trying to get to know him. I should be asking for his number, not writing messages about Canada.

And that's pathetic, isn't it? I am completely changing what I do just so she'll ignore me. That's not wise. It's dumb.

I think about all this during history and miss some key points about World War I. This makes me feel completely guilty, because clearly it was totally dreadful and really mattered.

The end-of-school bell charges me out of a total spiral of worry. Lauren rushes over to me, brandishing her phone with a face of total fury. "LOOK! HOW. Does. SHE. Do. It?!"

I look. There for all to see and already with thirty-two likes is a selfie of Erin and Danny. It's a fantastic aerial shot. She's obviously used her selfie stick and her phone cover with backlighting. The filter makes them even better-looking than normal.

Erin has captioned the picture:

Welcome to @DannyTruds from Ontario #NewBoy
Thank you, Danny, for letting me post this cute selfie!

And let me tell you all, my new BBF (Best Boy Friend,
before you ask) is a keeper ;) Remember, girls,
#StrongMen like #StrongWomen, and don't be too shy
to make a boy your friend #Feminism

"Can you even believe it?" Lauren says. "The truth is, no one
has been more evil to you or to me than Erin Breeler. If being a feminist means you are nice to all women, then she is not one."

I don't think feminism means that. It means we as females believe
we are entitled to be treated equally and ought to have the same
opportunities as men. And that we should not be judged completely
on our looks.

Lauren has a different point of view. "Well, I think it should be
about being nice to women. And if it's about not being judged JUST
on how we look, then I am not taking anything from a woman who
has an Instagram account about how pretty she is!"

Lauren does have a point there, but Erin has SLAIN us on this
one. She bags Mr. Beautiful Boy AND gets to sound like a cool and
independent woman who doesn't look at secret photos of men's bums
and is great at life advice.

"One good thing," Lauren shouts excitedly, "is that it's completely
fine to stare at his photo now. *Danny Trudeau.* He sounds like an
amazing brand of car tire that would never let you down in any sort
of terrain! He's way out of our league, Millie."

Lauren is right, but this makes me cross. "Why is he? We're
attractive, funny, clever, modern women. He'd be lucky to go out
with either of us."

I don't believe this, but as Aunty Teresa says, fake it till you make it.

"Yes, Millie." Lauren rolls her eyes. "There is no doubt in my mind that you're going to end up married to him."

This is Erin's fault. She makes Lauren sarcastic and me either frightened or ridiculous.

Lauren doesn't need to say it. We all know who he'll end up going out with. Erin might be pretending that she's got a new guy friend, but we know her game. No way is she letting him out of her sight now. She'll share the picture of their first official coffee, their first time at the cinema, and the first lovely photo of them under a really nice tree with lots of dramatic branches. That's real life. That's how it works. We'll get to see their entire annoying love affair all in the Valencia or Hefe filters. And of course I'm going to look. I know I shouldn't, but I will.

And yes, MASSIVE jealousy face. Jealousy and annoyance at horrible girls snogging lovely boys IS common sense and right and would probably be approved by any sensible leader of any sensible country.

#Shook

When I get home from school, both Mum and Gary are waiting for me in the front room. I give MUM a hug. She looks at me with one of her eyebrows firmly planted on the ceiling and says, "Hello, Millie. Next time you come around, can you make sure I'm there? It would be lovely to actually speak to you."

I'm rumbled. "How did you know I was there?"

"Gary sensed a disturbance." Mum looks annoyed, and Gary looks distressed. "He felt there was something slightly out of place . . . and you accidentally locked the robot vacuum in your room when you left and closed the door behind you. It was going berserk. Like a trapped dog. Gary was very concerned."

Gary says seriously, "His little motor was a bit scorched, but he had a little rest and everything is okay."

I think I am meant to be relieved at this. The truth is, McWhirter is one of the few things in the world I am *not* worried about.

Betrayed by McWhirter. Lauren wasn't paranoid—she was right. That hoover has totally got it in for us. Mum carries on. She sounds hurt, too.

"Why did you come around when we were both out? Come on,

Millie! I know you. I know it wouldn't have been for something stupid, but . . . have things got so bad that you can't see me? What did you want to hide from me?"

What do I say? It was for something Mum would never understand and she wouldn't even want to try to understand. She'd be furious if I told her about the vlog.

I say, "Oh, I'd just forgotten my . . . onesie. It's really cold here, Mum. They don't really—"

"I know!" Mum interrupts. "You can come home, you know. Your dad's a good man, but he lives in a way that's very different from what you're used to. You make good choices, Millie. And choices are what LIFE is all about. You need to make thoughtful and considered ch—"

Mum is disturbed midsentence by the sound of a mad car honking. We rush to the front door, and pulling into the drive is a very battered and old ice-cream truck. Teresa leans her head out of the driver's window and starts shouting, "I am Mrs. Whippy! Hear me ROAR."

"It's the greatest idea ever!" she yells. "I just need to get the fridges fixed, the motor tweaked a bit, and the thing that plays the tune installed, but I don't really *need* that—I can just shout 'ICE CREAM!' out the window. I mean, at the moment, it can only go about five miles per hour, but you don't need to go that fast when you're an ice-cream truck anyway, do you? I'm sure people won't mind waiting behind me. Everyone loves ice cream. Also, it's the greatest way ever to meet guys!"

At this point, Teresa finally spots my mum and Gary. "Oh, hello! How are you? Fancy sponsoring me? Seriously, this is a cast-iron business opportunity. This is a family business that can be passed down through generations!"

Mum doesn't reply to Teresa. She just looks at me and says sternly, "Choices. Decisions, Millie."

Mum can always find things to prove her point. They land in her lap. Even bad old ice-cream vans.

"Anyway," Mum continues. "Look. You're welcome at the house anytime, and, Millie—you can tell me anything. You know that. That's how we work, you and me. Honesty. You normally make the right decisions. Please try to keep on doing that."

Gary starts violently sneezing and says, "Can we go? This place is terrible for my allergies. And yes, Rachel, I've had a squirt of my nasal spray, but even that can't perform miracles."

Mum gives Teresa a hug and says, "When you get it going properly, give me a call." Mum knows Teresa never will, but Mum isn't nasty. She's ace. Really annoyingly ace and sensible—just living with a man who knows I was cruel to his hoover. He will never forgive me and will probably report me to the Royal Society for the Prevention of Cruelty to Vacuum Cleaners.

Mum then gives me one of those hugs that I never want to end. But it does end, and she goes back to my house. Her house. Gary's house. Probably just McWhirter's house. It doesn't matter. It makes me feel like I want to put a duvet over my head and eat biscuits.

I leave Teresa and Dad downstairs to plan their gourmet ice-cream van business and lie on my bed. Erin now has over five hundred likes for her photo. It is perfect. Danny is perfect. The comments say stuff like:

Gorgeous!

Your attitude is so inspiring ☺

A true #Feminist #Warrior

I mean, WHAT?! These people don't really know Erin. They see her photos and think she is beautiful inside and out, but she's . . .

The fact is, I am jealous. And actually, there is a lot to learn from Erin. She takes what she does online really seriously. She plans it and filters it and takes every photo a hundred times and writes things that people love. Things that she KNOWS people will love. I can't do that because I haven't got her arch-nemesis-brain of evil genius, but I can take what I need to do seriously.

That's what I need to do.

I message Lauren.

Lauren. When we do this vlog, we are doing it RIGHT.

She messages me back with:

Learn from Bradley, Mills. He's a genius with it all.

She is right. The Emperor of Escalators is the key to my success.

#Butterflies

Saturday morning comes around and I'm feeling really nervous. The weird thing is, it's like a date sort of nervous. When I went out with Dylan Anthony, I used to feel like this. I was worried about kissing wrong and garlic breath. But none of that matters with Bradley. He's a sweet guy, but I don't *like him* like him. And as for Danny? No chance. I need to tell my head that. . . .

Dear Brain,

Just because there is now no chance of you going out with Danny, it does not mean that there will be tongues with Bradley Sanderson. It's just going to be escalators and vlogging advice. Get over yourself. He's got a girlfriend. Stop getting in a tizz. Stop creating a spiral of total doom and—

"Where are you going, and why are you talking to yourself?" Granddad stops me by the front door. His fingernails are full of mud.

"I'm meeting my new friend Bradley." I tell him the truth. I don't want to, though, as I know where it will lead.

"Oh!" Granddad is teasing me now. He winks and does a tiny jump. Actually, it's more of a raise of his heels. That's all he can manage. "A young man? Is this your boyfriend?"

Why do girls always have to go through this with family members whenever they mention a male?

"He's JUST a friend!"

"Of course he is!" Granddad does his annoying wry smile.

"You realize you can actually be friends with a boy, Granddad? Just friends. You don't have to marry them. You can just meet them and chat!"

Granddad harrumphs. The problem is, I do sound a bit lame. A boy is teaching me how to do stuff. I'm not particularly happy about this, and I'm certainly not letting Granddad know that. He still believes that men are the best natural teachers. He tells his own doctor what is wrong with him before she can explain. And he calls her "nurse," even though she is a doctor.

But he's letting me live in his house and use his shed, so I just smile and leave. This is not fighting for equality, but it is sensible.

That word again. Sorry. I can't help it.

ARGH! Why am I so nervous?

#LoveLifts

When I eventually find Bradley Sanderson in the shopping mall, he is standing inside a lift with his phone pointed at the control panel. It's lunchtime on a Saturday. The place is busy. A mum is trying to wheel her stroller in, but Bradley doesn't notice her. It's like he's totally in a world of his own.

He eventually sees me waiting outside the lift and says, "The first thing you need for successful vlogging, Millie, is focus. Focus. Ignore everyone else around you. They are irrelevant to your key mission."

"That's all very well," says the lady with the stroller, "but Oliver and I need to get to the florist's on the first floor."

Bradley scowls at her, presses a button, and whips out through the doors just before they close.

"People who use these lifts don't understand the beauty of them— the thought that has gone into all the engineering. They just use them to go up or down. It makes me cross. Anyway, YOU. I've been think-ing about your vlog. Shall we go and have a coffee?"

This is really sweet. Bradley has been thinking about me and actually wants to talk to me properly. I get the feeling that he doesn't think about people in general very much. I feel a bit . . . honored.

"Planning, Millie Porter!" Bradley continues once we've got a chai latte (me) and a green tea (Bradley). I insist on paying. It's the twenty-first century, and this is NOT a date. "You want to bring something to your audience that they need to hear or haven't heard before. Something different. Don't assume that you are the only one that feels something. I used to be embarrassed about liking lifts, but then I found out that all over the world there were lift lovers like me. And if it's not hurting anyone, then it's FINE. What advice exactly do YOU want to give?"

"I want to help people. I want to put this boring brain of mine to good use for a change but not be boring with it. But. Yeah. I do. I want to help people who feel . . . BAD. I've been finding it a bit hard with my mum's new boyfriend and my best friend is having all sorts of trouble with her parents."

I feel stupid saying all this, especially to a nerdy boy in ninth grade, but it's true.

Bradley seems to speak more softly. It's like he's starting to care . . . a bit.

"Well, you need to THINK about what you are going to say, then. You have to find a way to be different. To stand out."

"What about how it looks?" I ask.

Bradley stares at me through his glasses. "Shock! Horror!" he says. "That doesn't matter as much as what you say."

"It does to girls." I feel dreadful saying this, but I have a terrible feeling that it might be true.

"I don't know about girls. Not many women are into lifts."

"Don't be sexist, Bradley." I snap at him a bit.

"It's not sexist, Millie. It's actual fact. And anyway, you just said girls are basically only interested in how things look! That's definitely sexist."

There's a bit of a pause. I fiddle with my sugar wrapper.

Then Bradley rather casually says, "I actually think Hashtag Help is an okay idea. I'm not too keen on the name. It's a bit . . . try-hard cute. I don't do cute. But I reckon you could find an audience if you keep it down-to-earth. To be honest, there are times when I would watch a vlog like that."

I'm surprised Bradley is admitting this. "I didn't ever think you would need something like that." This is rather a massive lie. Sometimes massive lies are good.

Bradley knows I'm just being nice. "It's not easy being me. I might have thousands of subscribers and my own channel, but it can't have escaped your notice, Millie, that I don't really fit in at school."

I don't know what to say here. It's very true, and I can't pretend it's not.

An "Um. Well . . ." is all I can manage.

"It's like my vlogs: I edit out all the people calling me 'weirdo' and 'geek' and 'lift lover' and the bits when I get pushed out of the way."

Bradley looks really sad at this point. I start to feel a bit bad for the number of times Lauren and I have laughed at him.

I don't really know what to say, but Bradley saves me by talking about my vlog again.

"Your vlog could be useful. It would be good to be able to ask someone who is a real person AND who is the same age and not get a massive lecture about what I should and shouldn't do. Anonymously, naturally. I don't want to be talked about. Or talked about in the bad way." He's smiling at me as he says this.

The bad way, of course, is people saying you aren't a hottie or that you're weird or a freak. If I'm going to be honest, I doubt anyone talks much about Bradley at all, and if they do, I doubt it's in a good way. Which is bad really, because when you spend time with him, you realize he's actually . . . sort of . . . kind, I suppose. I'm dreading asking the next question, but I know I have to.

"Did you see the cat vlog Lauren and I did?"

"Yeah." Bradley scrunches his face up.

"Thoughts?"

"It was fun," Bradley says. His face is still scrunched up.

"And . . . ?" I ask.

"Okay, Millie. I'm going to be straight with you." He unscrunches his face a tiny bit. "It was fun . . . and that's it. It was a laugh. But everybody is sort of over that, Millie. Cats were big about three years ago. And anyway, that kind of content isn't real life. It's like a perfect edited piece of it. Cats are just dull most of the time, but if you believed what you saw online, you would think everyone had a perfect, ugly, trampolining pet. Did you know some really popular vloggers and Instagrammers are quitting because it's got too fake? You can start living your life to fit the vlog. Everything becomes about online. And really good life and lifts can pass you by. I ignored a paternoster once because I didn't think people on the vlog would be interested. I regret it now."

I don't know what a paternoster is, but I get his point, and it's a bit of a revelation. I hadn't really thought about it in quite that way before.

"You know what, Bradley," I say. "I AM going to be real. I'm going to have fun but be real. Talk about real stuff. Talk about what it's REALLY like. Tell the TRUTH and look REAL and . . . natural. I'm not going to wear lots of makeup, either. But there's only one problem: If I go completely natural and real, I will be trolled into a coma."

Bradley laughs softly. "Millie. You'll get trolled anyway. I can't pretend you won't. Just do it. People will always find fault with you. Do you think it's easy loving lifts? It's not. I'm a lift-loving cosplayer. We are basically a very-easy-to-laugh-at minority group. But who cares? Now, I've got to go and see if I can get some footage of the inner workings. It's been . . . really . . . quite okay speaking to you. Just go and do it. Yeah, just . . . be you."

And with that, Bradley quickly gets up and dashes up the stairs that are there for people who are terrified of lifts.

I stand there feeling like I've been with one of the wisest, sweetest, weirdest people on the planet. He shouldn't live under coats. He should spread all that brain everywhere and not just on escalators. Also, he said very lovely things about me, which makes me feel . . . odd.

I need to get back to Lauren before I forget all the good advice he's given me. I think we are ready to start #Help.

#DictatorHair

I get the bus from the mall to Lauren's house. The whole time, I'm thinking about Bradley.

When Lauren lets me in, she seems really confused. "I'm reading something that someone shared. They want hair like a young Joseph Stalin, but they don't want to show a photo of Stalin to the hairdresser."

I am very used to Lauren being a bit "out there," but this is seriously random, even for her.

"And . . . ?" I ask.

Lauren stares at me. "What's so wrong with Stalin?"

Where to start? I spend the next five minutes explaining that Stalin killed everyone who didn't agree with him, that millions starved when he was in control, and that, generally, he was completely horrible with a really bad mustache.

Lauren listens to all this and then holds up her phone and shows me a photo. "But, to be fair, he was really cute when he was younger. Look! He could be in a boy band."

There is absolutely no doubt that Stalin, when he was younger, was quite attractive, but it all comes back to what Bradley says. How much stuff should we let people get away with in real life because they are cute and take a good photo? I'm feeling quite—what word does Mum use?—*militant* about this.

Lauren interrupts my thoughts. "Anyway. What did the escalator-geekathon say?"

"Don't call him that!" My reaction takes me by surprise. I feel a bit protective of Bradley now.

Lauren looks at me. "Millie. I would be amazed if Bradley Sanderson didn't seriously fancy you! I mean, how many NON-dates do you think he goes on?"

"Lauren!" I snap. "It was NOT a date, and he does NOT fancy me. We're just friends. He has a girlfriend. He can help me, and we can both . . . have a good time."

Lauren drops her phone and shrieks, "YOU fancy Bradley Sanderson!"

"No!" And I really don't. "But he knows his stuff, Lozza. He says planning is the key. And he thinks that the vlog should be REALLY honest and talk about stuff that properly affects people. And"—I sort of say this really quickly—"I shouldn't wear too much makeup."

Lauren is startled. "Everybody wears makeup in vlogs and in life, Millie. It's one of the world's lovely things."

Lauren has gone pale. I can see it even through her foundation.

"Lauren, I don't think that no makeup is a bad idea. In one of the vlogs, I want to talk about how you don't want to go online because of how you look. I won't say your name! I'll just talk about how to be more confident and what to do if people call you names. And just by me not wearing makeup, it makes the point that it's real and I believe what I say."

Lauren has gone even paler. There is now probably not even a shade of foundation in existence that matches her skin tone.

"Millie, I'm worried about you." Lauren puts her arm around me. "This is basically an invite to every troll in the world. It's like walking up to Mr. Style Shame and saying, 'Come into my bedroom and call me a dork.'"

I remember what Bradley said about everybody getting trolled, whatever they do.

"I can handle it," I say.

At that point, an odd sound starts downstairs. It sounds like a thunderstorm.

Lauren notices that I'm a bit concerned.

"Don't worry, Mills. When my dad gets really cross with my mum, he does a drum solo on the radiators with forks. Their marriage counselor said it was a good way to ease the tension."

I hear Lauren's dad shout, "I'm only here because of her!"

Lauren sighs. "He also does that. A lot."

I don't know what to say. Which is every shade of useless.

Lauren must sense this, because she hugs me and says, "Let's get together in the shed tomorrow. Let's do it. I'm there for you every step of the way—as long as I can be off-screen with defined brows and a decent lippy."

"I love you, Lauren. You're brilliant. Just please don't marry a Russian dictator."

Rubbish jokes are all I can manage sometimes. She smiles, and I leave. Her parents don't notice. Her dad is playing the kitchen cabinets and her mum has turned the TV up to a volume level that even Granddad could hear.

#Help is happening. Lauren is ready. I'm ready. I think.

I think I am. *Can* I handle it, though? Can I handle people calling me stuff?

I hope I can delete it from my head.

When I get back to Granddad's, I start to plan what I'm going to say. I write down a few notes. I'd like to talk to Dad about it, but he's not here. To be honest with you, he's hardly ever here. He's mainly somewhere else arranging something else. When I lived with Mum, she was there even when she wasn't. If I needed her, she would usually magically appear. I miss that. . . .

Okay, yes! I miss HER.

Anyway. I can't think about all that now. I have to be clear in my head about what I want to say and where I want things to go. I need to keep focusing forward. Moving up like a . . . lift.

No. You can stop thinking that, too. I do NOT fancy Bradley. I do, however, love someone who is just proud to be who they are and gets on with it. Hurrah for escalators . . .

In a way.

#RealVlogOne

Lauren and I are in the Shed of Vlog. It's Sunday morning, and Granddad has taken down his calendar. This is a small but sweet act of loveliness on his part. Now everyone will know we have nothing to do with wading birds.

Lauren moves a spade out of the way and looks at me. "Are you ready, Mills?"

I tell her yes. I've been practicing all night in the mirror. I think I've got it. I've planned my advice, and I've planned how to say it. I've nicked a bit of it from stuff I've seen in magazines, but I think I can get away with it.

Lauren counts me in like a proper film director. "Three. Two. One. ACTION!"

"Hello. I'm Millie, and welcome to the very first Hashtag Help vlog! You can see that I'm doing this without any makeup on. Extreme close-up please, Lauren."

(And Lauren zooms the phone RIGHT in so you can basically dive into my pores.)

"And the truth is, I'm really scared, because no makeup means—"

(At this point, we hear a very loud, odd version of "Humpty Dumpty Sat on a Wall.")

"Ignore that! That's my aunty Teresa. She bought an ice-cream van and just got the siren thingy going. She hasn't got any freezers, but she's working on that.

"Um, where was I? Okay, I just want to explain why I'm doing this without any contouring or stuff. I love makeup, but there are things that are more important than eyeliner. I didn't want to be all shallow and for my vlog to just be about how I look.

"Anyway, today I want to talk to you about parents. 'Hashtag Help Me Cope With Crazy Adults In My Life.' We are always told that anyone over the age of eighteen should know what they're doing. The fact is, they don't. As you can hear, my aunty Teresa has bought a mobile dessert truck. I wish I could say this was the first time she's done something random like this, but it's not. And I don't think she's going to change. In fact, as long as the adults in your life are not actually hurting you, you kind of have to accept that they are very unlikely to change. If they are the sort of people who are convinced that they invented synchronized swimming in a kiddie pool at the age of four, then they're probably going to be the same at forty-four.

"Accept them, and, if you can, try to help them. For example, my aunty Teresa has said that she's going to make an avocado-and-chili-ripple ice cream for her van, and I've very gently steered her to peanut butter and caramel. You can make a difference to people's lives . . . and people's desserts.

"Now, coping with random adults is less difficult than coping with parents. Parents expect more of you, so they are basically a different species. I have lovely parents, but my mum is currently going out with a man who

thinks that a vacuum cleaner's feelings are worth more than mine. So I'm living with my dad. He is great, but he's not around that much.

"Generally with parents, I think that the following FOUR things are good to do:

1. *Tell them where you are going. If you just disappear somewhere, they get really upset. If your parents watch a lot of crime shows, like CSI, this will definitely be the case, as they think really clever murderers live in mailboxes on every street.*
2. *Occasionally—and I know it's hard—start a conversation with them about school. This makes them stupidly happy and they'll stop asking you all those questions about your day, so it's a massive win-win situation thing.*
3. *Ask them about what they were like as teenagers. They might be weird about this to start with, BUT you could see a really surprising, human side of them. They may have had snogging issues or have been dumped horrifically. Remember, most of them didn't have a mobile phone till they were twenty-something, so their stories could be unbelievable. My mum once waited in a park for over an hour when her friend was meant to be meeting her. Her friend had actually been in a nasty homemade-Rollerblade accident in her own garden and couldn't walk. She wasn't horribly injured or anything, but no one could tell Mum. Her friend had a hedge and a wheel on her head, and Mum was completely in the dark, sitting in a park eating chips. Our parents had it really tough. You've got to give them a bit of love for that.*

4. *Okay, this step is harder. I have a friend whose parents argue loads but are staying together because of her. We all know that is just the worst idea ever. It would be far better for them to just call it a day and . . . Anyway . . . if you're living with adults who yell a lot, just—I know this is hard, like, the HARDEST—but try to remember that this is not your fault. And I KNOW they always say that on TV and in books and in serious chats at school. But it's TRUE. Your parents are just tools. A good thing is to take them aside and say, 'Look— your arguing is really getting to me and making me feel awful.' If you tell them how you feel, it might just work. It might not. It could make it worse, but honesty's worth a try.*

"*So that's me, Millie, with 'Hashtag Help Me Cope With Crazy Adults In My Life.' Please leave your comments, and, um . . . until next time . . .*"

I try to make a hashtag with my hands. I'm not sure it works.

"*Hashtag Help me to help you!*"

Lauren presses STOP.

"What do you think?!" I ask her immediately.

Lauren pulls the sleeves of her shirt over her hands.

"How you say I should handle my parents in real life is different from what you've said there."

This is true. It is.

"I know," I say. "But I'm trying to be more general with things so it can help more people. Do you know what I mean?"

Lauren looks down at her hands. "Yeah," she sighs. "They are pretty unique. In a pretty bad way."

I try to get off the subject and cheer her up. "What did you think of the whole vlog?"

Lauren thinks hard. "Er. Good. For a first go. I think. Not, er, too preachy," Lauren says. "Are you going to upload that?"

She seems unsure. I stare at her.

"You know what, Lauren. I think I'm going to just think about it for a while. I think that's . . ."

And we both say it together:

"*Sensible*."

#Upload

I sit in my room for hours. I tidy everything about four times. I look underneath the bed and discover a box of My Little Ponies. I go on eBay to see how much they are worth. I find out they are worth nothing because Teresa has cut off their manes and written *Teresa is the best jockey ever* all over them. I brush Dave and then try to tie a small bow on her head. She attempts to eat it.

After all this, I still can't decide whether I should upload the vlog or not.

Eventually, I decide I need some advice about my actual advice vlog.

I track down Granddad. He's in his shed. He's put his calendar back up, and he's sawing a piece of wood. He does this a lot. You never get to see where the wood goes or what it does.

"Granddad, would you do something even if you thought people would laugh at you for it?"

Granddad stops sawing and sits down. "I married your grandma."

I hate it when he does this. Rubbish, ancient anti-women jokes. You need him to be helpful, and he just goes silly.

"Granddad! I'm serious!" I yell.

"So am I," he sighs. "You're old enough now, so I'll tell you something, but keep it to yourself. Your grandma was pregnant with Teresa when I met her."

My brain takes a second or two to process this. This is a major revelation. I had NO IDEA. "What?" I yelp. "So she isn't yours?!"

"She's mine," Granddad says firmly. "Blood isn't always thicker than love. Your grandma was seen as damaged goods years ago. People said, 'Don't marry her.' But she was lovely. She'd made a mistake. A man told her he loved her, and he didn't. I did. So I married her, and I didn't have a miserable day or a sandwich for dinner for thirty-five years. You've got to do what you think is right, Millie. Common sense—that's what you've got. Teresa hasn't got any, but at least she follows her heart. That's something. If YOU think that what you've got to say is worth hearing, then who cares what other people think? If it could help one person feel better, SHARE IT! But, Millie . . ."

And Granddad grabs my hand. "You HAVE to look after yourself. That's important. Now, get lost. I need to cut some wood."

Granddad may be harsh, but sometimes he gets it right.

That's it. I'm going to do it.

I call Lauren as soon as I close the shed door behind me.

"I'm with you," Lauren says, and that's JUST what I want to hear. "Can I come over? I'd quite like to get out of the house, and anyway, we *are* doing this together."

When Lauren arrives at the house, she's carrying a jar of celebratory chocolate-hazelnut dip. "Let's toast to our success with sweet grissini!" she shouts before shoving one in my mouth and laughing. It's a great friend that helps you AND brings you random sugar.

Just as we are about to press UPLOAD, my stomach suddenly goes into a panicked flutter. All the questions that have been rushing around my head all day suddenly seem all too real. What am I doing? What will Danny—or Bradley—think about it? What if Mum or Erin see it?

Dave chooses this moment to jump onto my laptop keyboard and attempt to steal a grissino.

She also presses UPLOAD.

Lauren looks at me. "Well, Mills, it's gone. Decision made. It's up. Hashtag it on ALL your accounts with hashtag real, hashtag vlog, hashtag makeup, hashtag feminism, hashtag advice, hashtag life, and anything else that is trending now, and let's see what happens!"

I agree with her but tell her that we should leave it for twenty-four hours before we even check the views. Otherwise, we'll just get down about it. New vlogs take time to build an audience. I read that in an article.

Lauren just puts her hugely serious face on and says, "This is history, Millie. This is gorgeous Stalin when he could be in a boy band. This is . . ."

At this point, Aunty Teresa bursts in, shouting, "Have you started a proper vlog, Mills?! Granddad mentioned you were doing something involving videos that everyone in the world can see. Brilliant! And perhaps, if it goes viral, you can ever so subtly put an advert in for my ice-cream van, too!"

Lauren catches my eye. We don't want to tell Teresa exactly what we've said about her.

"Let's see how it goes," I say.

I think I say this to Aunty Teresa quite a lot.

Aunty Teresa skips off to work on more ludicrous flavors of ice cream.

Lauren says to me very seriously, "How are you going to even sleep tonight now that it is out THERE?"

My tummy does a backflip. Perhaps I should give my phone to Lauren so I'm not checking it all night, but then . . . I know that I can just look at Dad's iPad. It will be impossible not to check. Impossible not to see how people react. Impossible not to . . . "Loz, it will be impossible."

"Millie!" Lauren shouts. "You're not a celebrity. Nothing will happen for hours. DON'T WORRY. This is a really fun thing we are doing. Don't spoil it!"

Lauren is right, but it's a bit of a major life-role reversal when she is the sensible one.

"I bet you can't stop yourself checking it!" I snap.

"Bet I can!" She laughs as she deletes the YouTube app off her phone and off mine, too.

"Lauren!" I yell. "This is INSANE!" And it is, but I feel like being totally insane.

"RIGHT! No checks till lunchtime tomorrow on any device! HASHTAG PINKIE PROMISE!" Lauren giggles as she curls her little finger around mine. This is our sacred bond. I can't break this. I think that if I do, something dreadful will happen.

It probably won't.

I hope.

I try to have an early night. Dave walks on my forehead, pleading with me to give her some tuna-flavor luxury cat snacks. It's hard to relax.

A MASSIVE part of me says this has been a terrible mistake. It may lead to glory, or it may lead to . . .

#ChemicalReaction

I spent last night reading too many articles about terrible diseases. But I managed not to look at the vlog. Now it's Monday morning, and I'm sitting in science with Lauren, watching Danny Trudeau.

And I'm not the only one. He's been picked to perform an experiment in front of the class. Never in the history of school anywhere in the world has potassium permanganate been put on a dish so perfectly. The way Danny picks up a spatula is poetry. He follows instructions on the whiteboard with tiny glimpses and, without even looking properly, manages to scoop just the right amount. Danny Trudeau: Scoop Master. If this were a YouTube video, the comments section would be all heart emojis and jealous scientists saying they could do it better. They couldn't.

"Mills," whispers Lauren, "he's about to add the glycerin. In a few minutes, we'll see the fire. The true fire of Trudeau."

This makes us both giggle a lot. I don't know what it is, but there's something about Danny starting a small chemical explosion that is just about taking my mind off my vlog. It has been itching around in my brain now for hours. All night. ALL day. I am desperate to see how many views we've had, what comments we've got, who has seen it, and who hasn't seen it. Now I FINALLY have the perfect distraction. Doctor Danny and his spatula of love.

After the lesson, Lauren and I are walking behind the Canadian scientist of dreams and I realize I have the perfect opportunity to talk to him about something clever. I understand everything that just happened. I paid TOTAL attention to all of it. It's like things have all come together to make this one moment. It's like . . .

It's like Bradley Sanderson is straight in front of my face. Completely blocking the view of Danny's brilliant, atoms-changing body.

"I saw it," he says. "I saw your vlog."

There are two problems here. I really want to see Danny, but I also want to hear what Bradley thought about the vlog.

"What did you think?" I ask. I try to split my eyes to keep one on him and one on Trudeau's magic. It doesn't work. I just go cross-eyed.

Bradley stares at me hard. "It's really, really . . . brave."

I find this a bit worrying. The way Bradley says "brave" doesn't make it feel like a massive compliment. In fact, it makes me feel like I'm doing something really stupid—like riding a bike over a really tall cliff with just a big shirt as a parachute.

Bradley can see my face has slightly collapsed and tries to reassure me. "No. I thought it was, like—honest and fresh. I showed my mum, and she really liked it."

Lauren nudges me in the ribs and makes *I told you so* eyebrows.

"Great! Mums like it!" My sarcasm explodes with more fizz than Danny's experiment. I feel instantly bad, though. Bradley seems almost hurt.

I go all enthusiastic. "How come you saw it? Did you go hunting for it?"

Bradley looks down and sideways and up and everywhere eyes can possibly go. "Er. No. That girl in your year who's always posting on Instagram shared it."

Lauren and I stare at each other.

Oh no. This is not good.

Danny has stopped to talk to someone. We walk past him. He grins in our general direction. If I wasn't feeling so worried, I could almost think he was smiling JUST at me. But that's the thing about my anxiety—it changes the entire world and how I see everything. He was probably just generally happy at making a small bomb that teachers approve of.

I want to go to the Zen Loo and check my phone immediately, but I can't. I have to sit through half an hour of Mrs. Caldwell going on about binary code. I usually love Mrs. Caldwell and her amazing glasses that have interchangeable color inserts for different days of the week, but I NEED to see what Erin has said.

An Erin takedown could take me down. FOREVER.

#MeanGirl

As soon as the lesson ends, I rush to the Zen Loo to scroll through Erin's Instagram. She's posted a link to my vlog and a selfie of herself made up in her usual perfect way. She's tilted her head to the screen, there's metallic shadow on her eyelids, and her lips are red. It shouldn't work, but it's Erin, and it does. She's written:

> There's a really interesting new vlog called #Help @MilliePorter that basically says people who like makeup are shallow. Girls, I don't think another girl should tell you what you can or can't do. Are you with me? I think it's empowering to use makeup to make the best of your features. If you are anti-makeup, you are anti-freedom, anti-girl, and anti-feminist. #Feminist #GIRLPOWER #Makeup #Eyes #Lips

I don't even bother to check my vlog. I take the biggest breath possible, leave the bathroom, and show it to Lauren. She's standing with Bradley. Lauren puts her arm around me. Bradley puts his arm around me, too. What is going on?!

I manage to blurt out, "That's not what I said at all. I just said that . . ."

"Look, Millie," Bradley says matter-of-factly, despite the fact that he's still got his arm around me. "To Erin, you've basically declared war. ANYONE who does anything half decent on social media threatens her. Unless it's about lifts. BUT she's also given you loads of publicity that you wouldn't have had otherwise."

Bradley is peering at me through his huge glasses in a way that makes me feel a bit confused. He's sweet. And reassuring. And Lauren is looking at us both VERY suspiciously.

"Also, Millie, I, er . . . I, er . . . wanted to know if you wanted to meet up on Saturday again—to discuss your next vlog?" Bradley continues, going quite red. "I know it doesn't seem like the world of escalators and the world of problem-solving have a lot in common, but I think that after seeing your . . . thing . . . that I know a way you could reach *even more* people."

I can't believe I am saying this, but I agree and tell Bradley that Saturday sounds lovely. Bradley immediately rushes off, doing his usual cling-to-the-wall disappearing act.

After what's happened today, I need all the help I can get. I know I've got Loz, but she's not an expert. And she's currently exploding, grinning from ear to ear.

"Now, Millie," she whispers, "you can't say that is not a date! He totally, utterly likes you, NOT JUST IN THE FRIEND WAY! He put his arm around you!"

I'm about to yell at Lauren about the difference between professional business meetings and dates when Danny Trudeau taps me on the shoulder.

"Hi, Lauren! Hi, Millie! I liked Hashtag Help. Nice work! It's good to know that I'm not the only one with a weird family. My dad is currently trying to build a model tank from scrap metal. He's been watching too many killer-robot movies and is prepping for their takeover."

I play it cool. "Do you know what sort of tank?"

Danny shuffles his feet, tilts his head slightly, and says, "Kinda big. Gray. Noisy when you're chilling. Are you a weaponry expert, Millie?"

He beams at me. All of a sudden, I feel slightly hilarious in the good way.

"Not really. I know a lot about Nerf guns. I can SLAY with a Nerf gun."

Danny looks me square in the face. "Now THAT I would love to see," he says.

There is a huge, drive-a-bus-through-it uncomfortable gap. Am I meant to say, "I would love to have a pretend battle with you!" or "Anytime!"? In the end, just to break the silence, I blurt out, "I'm not really good with Nerf guns. In fact, I've never tried one."

I don't know why I say this. Danny looks a bit sad.

"Anyway," he drawls, "I'm gonna do what you suggested: not try to change Dad. Just accept him. Even though he fired a toy grenade at me when I was doing my homework last night! It was a good vlog, though. I liked it. Gotta go. Bye, guys."

Once he's gone, Lauren and I turn to each other.

"Don't, Millie," Lauren snaps. "You've already got Bradley fancying you. Danny is ERIN PROPERTY. Don't you DARE mess with him. He will be the icing on the cherry."

Lauren means "the icing on the cake." Danny Trudeau is out of bounds. I know it. Lauren knows it. Instagram knows it. THE WORLD knows it.

We hear a lovely dressage-horse clopping sound. Erin swishes by us and breezily calls out, "Hey, Millie! You know, I could see what you were trying to do: something powerful and . . . real. Only, it didn't quite come off, did it? You just looked a bit . . . tragic. Still, there's time to get good. Keep working on it! Danny, wait!"

And Erin catches up with Danny. I see his face light up. Erin flicks her phone out to show him something. I look at Lauren. Surely they are dating. It is inevitable.

"The Danny cake is burnt, Millie. Move away," Lauren sighs.

The Queen has bagged her Prince, and I'm Cinderella with a vlog in a shed and no Fairy Godmother.

#Comments

On the way home from school, Lauren and I _finally_ read all the comments underneath my vlog. It has nearly five hundred views. Not terrible.

The comments? Er . . . they're . . . mixed.

> Good advice . . . if you are stupid

> This helped with Mum, thanks!

Okay, this is a nice person who deserves a response.

> Don't talk about things that you don't understand

> OMG pretty gurl

> #Angst

> Bit weird but quite good really

Who do you think you are stupid cow?

Lose 34lbs a week on the guava diet

Why are you in a shed? LOL

Respect from Brazil!

Hot. How old are you ;)

Are you a feminist? Is that why you are bare-faced?

I take a few deep breaths.

"Mills! Don't be sad, that's a really good question!" Lauren says. "Answer that and also say you're not being anti-makeup. You're just saying it is fine not to wear makeup."

Between you and me, I'm feeling a bit flat and angry. Erin has managed to twist everything I have said, ignore the main bit of advice about insane adults, and make it somehow all about her. AGAIN.

I start ranting at Lauren. "You know, next time I will do half of it in makeup and half not and that will shut EVERYONE UP!"

Lauren stops us both dead in the street. "Hang on, though. That could be a great idea."

I gape at her. "If I do that, EVERYONE will think I'm a complete and utter idiot. Everyone will be talking about it. Everyone . . ."

Hang on. When you think about it, it's the most perfect way to make my point. This is actually a fantastic idea.

"LAUREN"—I hug her tight—"YOU ARE A GENIUS!" We dance up and down outside McDonald's for a bit.

Lauren nods her head, very proud of herself. "I'll do one side of your face made up and one side not. You'll look great both ways. Everyone will love you. You will answer Erin without deliberately going for her. Feminism and makeup will be saved. You may even become a sensation."

And then she gives me some serious head-swaying sass. "And now you think Bradley is the vlogging BOMB—"

"Well, er, yes, but no, but . . . bye, Lauren! See you tomorrow!"

I quickly run away before she can ask me anything more. Perhaps wanting to see Bradley ISN'T just about vlogging. Perhaps I am having major feelings for someone brainy and sweet and perhaps . . .

When I get to our street, I see that Mum is waiting on Granddad's front porch. She is not happy.

It's very easy to lose the ability to talk when my mum is giving The Stare.

"Millie," she says as she guides and sort of pushes me into the house. "We NEED to talk. NOW."

#Lecture

I take Mum to my bedroom. I've managed to push nearly everything left of Aunty Teresa's underneath the bed, including her wooden stable and play food that she can't bear to throw out because it reminds her of her first play set for horses. Not many horses I've met like plastic pizzas, but there is no point arguing with Aunty Teresa.

Mum sits on the end of the bed. "Your dad called me, Millie."

I look at her. That *is* surprising.

"I've heard about this because Granddad told your dad, who told me . . ." She corrects herself. "In fact, I've *seen* that you've become one of these people on the Internet who films themselves. And you talked about Gary and me!"

"I didn't!" I shout.

"You spoke about Gary. It's not nice to talk about people behind their backs."

"I didn't say his name, Mum." I sound right AND calm.

"Millie. You know I don't like to be treated like an idiot."

Why, then, is she acting like one by living with one? I can win this argument EASILY.

"Don't worry, Mum," I say quietly, "I'm sure lots of people have

126

got a robot hoover that they treat like a child. No one will realize it's Gary."

Mum gets her strop face on and her voice gets higher. "You also know I don't appreciate sarcasm, Millie. And I'm worried about you. On the Internet, there are evil people pretending to be people who are really nice. They want to hurt you. I mean, do you know who you are talking to? Do you really?!"

I try not to be cross at Dad and Granddad. I try not to be cross at Mum. She is patronizing me to death, but I know it's because she loves me, so I keep calm.

"Mum, seriously! I am talking *to them*. They are not talking to me. I don't say where I live—not even the country I come from. I know what I'm doing."

Mum's face goes red. "Does it make you a target for really terrible people, though, Millie?"

I still keep calm. "I think you've been watching too many films with Liam Neeson, Mum. Honestly, I promise that if I had any worries, I would come to you. I always have, haven't I? Like that time when someone at school told me that Father Christmas took all your teeth away if you'd been naughty that year. I was sleeping facedown all December. Remember?"

"Well," Mum says, "to use that story, these Internet people, like Father Christmas, are basically coming down the chimney, and they—"

There! I knew she was going to overreact! I have to shut her down before I lose it.

"Mum. Honestly. I'm fine. And all the homework's still being done."

And it is—I make time. I've got time. I still haven't got an actual desk in this house, but I just use Aunty Teresa's TV-dinner *Despicable Me 3* tray.

"Oh, Millie . . ." Mum sounds a bit sad now. "I'm missing out on what you do. Come home. I know I can't make you. Please just remember that I AM HERE. ALWAYS. ALWAYS."

And she does her heart fist pump, where she bangs her chest and then pats mine.

This makes me want to cry.

My mum is lovely, really. I know I should be hating on her and loads of my friends don't get on with their mums, but mine is cool. Apart from the fact that she is going out with a really clean dictator. Like a lemon-fresh Stalin.

If you love someone, it's often better if you have different houses. It just sorts it ALL out. I may do a vlog on it.

"By the way," Mum asks me as we go downstairs, "where is your dad?"

"Oh, he's out doing some work."

Between you and me, I have absolutely no idea where he is. As per usual.

#Honest

After Mum's gone, I feel a bit down. It doesn't help that it's Monday, when you just feel like you've got so far to go till the weekend.

If I were doing an honest vlog tonight, this is what I would talk about:

1. Those comments really hurt. They sting inside and make me feel sick. I KNOW they shouldn't, but they do. And I want to keep the vlog going so Erin and all the haters don't win. BUT IT'S HARD.

2. My dad is never here! Granddad acts more like my dad. I see Dave the cat more than I see my own father—and she's always out doing the feline party thing. I know Dad loves having me here, but it's just like my mum said: Dad is completely . . . his own man. He is not a bad man. He is not a bad dad. If I were in trouble, I know he would be here for me. But in normal life, he just lets me get along with things, and he does his own thing, and I . . .

3. Okay, I'm only telling *you* this: I sort of miss a clean home and knowing people are going to be around when they say they will be. I don't miss McWhirter and CONSTANTLY being treated like an actual ball of fluff on laminate wood flooring, but I do miss all the . . . organization. The stuff that makes you feel safe and not . . . panicky. I AM SO DULL. If only the Neat Freak Gary Woolton would DISAPPEAR and take his special antistatic flat-screen wipes somewhere else.

4. I love Danny Trudeau, and I've got no chance. And this isn't me wanting you to say, "Of course you have, Millie!" in a fish-for-compliments special, because if you've seen Erin, you'd know what I mean. ZERO chance.

5. If all that wasn't enough, I'm confused about Bradley Sanderson. I didn't want to admit it to Lauren, but I think I like him. In what way, I don't even know. I need the sensible part of my head to detach from all the squiggled-spoon-confused bits and sort it out. Or I could tell Mum. But that would mean admitting that I can't really cope and I'm not that . . . clever. Or wise. Or anything my vlog claims.

So that's my honest vlog. But there's no way I want to share all this with the rest of the world right now. Just with you and Dave the cat, who is currently halfway up the curtain, swinging from side to side. To her, a curtain is just a fabric playground. She's probably only copying what Aunty Teresa has already done anyway.

#Makeover

"**Millie. Just admit it. You're going on a date with** Bradley Sanderson this weekend."

The Monday blues have gone and now it's Hashtag Help night. Lauren and I are just about to do another vlog (even though this makes my heart race). I also think Lauren might have realized that I'm finding the whole Bradley thing confusing. I'm not telling her that, though.

"It's NOT a date, Loz. Like the last one was not a date. It's a . . . meeting about how I can improve my marketing strategy."

"Come on, Millie." Lauren looks at me like she doesn't believe a word I'm saying. "It's seriously about YOU liking him. If you two had babies, they would be, like, the most clever, sensible babies in the world. They could be like . . . Mark Zuckerberg."

I can't handle this level of Lauren love talk, so I go factual instead. This is a great way to get her off her current track of randomness.

"Loz, did you know you can change your language to 'Pirate' on Facebook?"

This is old news, but I've hooked her in. We never use Facebook these days, so I could tell her anything. I can see Lauren's brain has gone into serious overdrive.

"Really, Millie? Why?"

"I don't know," I say. "The point is that I'm not having babies with Bradley Sanderson. He's got a girlfriend in the States who he's never met."

"But why would anyone want to talk like a pirate?" Lauren is in real brain pain now.

My slightly evil plan has worked. Lauren has been diverted by fact.

"Let's get prepared and do the vlog."

We spend the next two hours doing makeup, and it's magnificent. One side of my face has Erin-based levels of cosmetic PERFECTION. On the other side, there is NOTHING. I look like a spoon but a spoon with a FANTASTIC POINT.

Lauren counts me in, and I go OFF!

"Hello! Millie Porter here with Hashtag Help! This time it's 'Hashtag Help Me Understand Feminism.' Can I be a feminist and wear makeup? Well, I've done something a little bit special with the help of my BFF Lauren that I just want to share with you.

"I've done half my face like this . . ."

(I thrust my makeup-perfection side into the camera.)

"And half of it like this . . ."

(I show the entire world my bare face.)

"The point is that you can wear makeup, or not wear makeup. Both are great. YOU can do what you like. Feminism is not about eyeliner or what we look like. It is about us being judged on who we really are. It's about us not getting treated differently because we are girls. It's about us getting the same opportunities as men, whether we have smoky eyes or bare eyes. It's about

my granddad not assuming that I can cook because I'm female. I can't, and I don't want to. Well—I might want to when I'm older, but only because I might decide that I want to make something nice for ME that isn't baked beans. And that's the point—makeup is ABOUT DOING IT FOR YOU! Like making your lunch! You aren't doing it to please men. They don't even understand decent contouring. Generally.

"The world these days HAS evolved. Like dinosaurs. Well, not like dinosaurs, as they died out. Probably because they didn't embrace feminism.

"Anyway, LOOK—basically, if you're wearing makeup and having fun, brilliant. You're a feminist.

"If you're NOT wearing makeup and having fun, then congratulations. You're a feminist, too!"

(At this point, I flash my face from side to side again, so everyone gets the full effect of the makeup.)

"Thank you. Leave any comments underneath. Hashtag Help me to help you! Loving your work!"

Lauren gives me a massive thumbs-up.

"Mills! That was really good. I mean, the bit about the dinosaurs was a little random, but it sort of worked. Perhaps it wasn't a massive comet that wiped them out. Perhaps it was all the female stegosauruses killing off the male T. rexes in anger at their sexism, and it all just escalated and—"

"It was definitely a comet, Loz," I say. "Let's upload it. The world needs to see your makeup genius." I can't believe I'm just going for it.

Lauren stares at me. "Yes, the world does, Millie, but you do need to wash it off before your whole family thinks you've completely lost it."

Yet again, we've done the sensible swap. What is happening to me?

#Trolls

I wake up early the next day. It's difficult sleeping at the moment because I can't wait to look at what's happened to the vlog. In fact, I do check it a few times in the night because the South American crew is a bit behind us time-wise and I just want to see if not speaking Spanish or Portuguese makes a difference to my message.

Who am I kidding? This is a fight for school subscribers—not for global supremacy.

The good news is . . . my subs are growing. Over three hundred. And I've had more than 452 views. Erin gave me the most excellent piece of advertising ever by having a major dig at me.

The bad news is . . . the comments. They are mainly horrible.

> I have two pet dinosaurs that aren't getting on. What
> do you suggest?

(Okay, actual LOL!)

> Dweeb. Dog.

You think you're cool. What you know? Dweeby Dog.

Cute idea! Nice vlog ☺

Of course feminism is about how you look! Please
leave intelligent things to the grown-ups

I bet Germaine Greer and Caitlin Moran are quaking in
their boots!

(I think this is sarcastic.)

Only ugly girls are feminists

(CAN YOU BELIEVE PEOPLE LIKE THIS EVEN EXIST?!
TROLL!)

Offensive to REAL feminists

Ugly girl moans about men. Same old same old

You're ugly whatever. Put bag over head!

Okay. That one does really, really get to me. I look in the mirror.
No, I'm not Erin Breeler–standard (who is?), but I'm not ugly, either.
And so what if I was?! It's like what J. K. Rowling said—is fat
(or, in this case, ugly) really the worst thing we can be? It's not. It's

worse to be a nasty piece of work who goes out to make people feel horrible about themselves.

That isn't what J. K. Rowling said exactly, by the way. She said it better, but . . .

Ugly?

It HURTS. And I can't stop thinking about it. And the sensible side of me thinks it's just some troll spreading the hate, but this HUGE side of me says that all this vlogging is a terrible idea and Mum is completely right and I'm completely wrong.

Why would you write that stuff? I mean, why would you go out to make someone feel bad about themselves when they have done nothing to you whatsoever?

I call Lauren first thing in the morning.

"Have you seen the comment that says I'm ugly?"

"Oh, Mills! That is TOTALLY just a troll. Look at all the other comments! There are some NICE comments on there, too. What would you say to me? 'Don't focus on the twonk! Look at all the other lovely twonkless things!'"

This is true. My sensible self is rebounding back onto me. "What should I do next, Loz?"

Lauren's voice slightly collapses. "To be honest, Mills, I've got quite a lot to think about myself at the moment. After I got home last night, my dad accused my mum of fracking an entire cheesecake."

I'm trying to make a great vlog and I need Lauren's help, BUT what she's saying makes no sense. I snap at her a bit. "*Fracking* as in when you mine for gas and stuff?"

"Yeah!" Lauren sighs sadly. "He said she ate it like an industrial process. He just knows what will really wind her up. The way she looks, the way she snores, the way she eats . . ."

I try to get her back on what we were talking about: my vlog and me getting trolled into trolldom and beyond. We both know we can't fix her parents.

"You realize what your biggest problem is, Millie? It's Erin. Yesterday I heard from lovely Gracie that Erin's thinking of launching a style vlog. If you ask me, that's definitely a revenge vlog attack. Anyway, see you at school in a bit."

As soon as I'm off the phone with Lauren, I check Erin's Instagram. Sure enough, she's posted the most gorgeous selfie ever with:

> **NEWS of an exciting new partnership with some**
> **people I KNOW you will love. Plus something**
> **you've always wanted! And I promise it's not going**
> **to involve garden sheds ;) It's just going to be**
> **COMMITTED TO GORGEOUS #ComingSoon**

Her friend Miranda has commented:

> **Can't wait, E! Will make a change from some**
> **DULLSVILLE preachy channels ;)**

This feels like a war now. I don't want it to be a war. I want it to be a peace. A big piece of peace. Perhaps Bradley will have some suggestions about what to do. There must be rival escalator vlogs that want to bring him down.

That wasn't meant to be a bad up-down joke, by the way. Even though it was.

Sorry.

#Date

Meeting Bradley in the shopping center on Saturday, again, starts off sort of weirdly.

We meet by his favorite lift, and the first thing I notice is that he's looking really good. And the fact that I think he looks good takes me by surprise. He's got a Star Wars T-shirt on with a jacket, and it sort of works. "I was going to do the full cosplay Vader on you." He smiles. "But I decided that committed dark side isn't really your style."

This makes me giggle. "The truth is, Bradley, if you want to turn up as FULL Jedi Knight, I don't really care."

Bradley sort of spins from side to side and laughs. "Surely you wouldn't want me to be Yoda."

"At least Yoda is wise," I say. I like Yoda. I don't know much about Star Wars, but I know he talks a lot of sense.

"So you'd prefer your men, Millie, to be two feet tall, old, green, and to talk in object-subject-verb word order?"

I stare at him hard. "I'll be honest, Bradley. I don't know what you mean."

"Nor do I, really," Bradley admits. "I looked it up on Wikipedia.

I've noticed that if you tell people things you've read on Wikipedia with a really straight face, everyone thinks you're really clever. For example, did you know that people with blue eyes are much more likely to have an accident involving trousers that don't fit properly than people with brown eyes?"

"Really?" This is an amazing statistic and one I could use in a vlog. It's good advice for getting dressed.

"It's totally made up," Bradley says. "I've also noticed that people believe everything I say because I'm a smart nerd with glasses."

This is actually really quite funny. I laugh, and I see Bradley crack a tiny smile. It's sweet.

"I'll tell you what is true." Bradley goes serious again. "More people die from taking selfies than are eaten by sharks."

"Honestly?" I squeal. "Wow. What would happen if sharks got the ability to take selfies themselves?"

Bradley thinks hard. "I suppose fatalities would skyrocket. People would take selfies with sharks because it was cool and then they'd be eaten."

This is the most bizarre conversation I've had in a very long time (and my BFF is Lauren), but I am really enjoying it.

Bradley and I go for a coffee. I let him pay this time. It's only fair. And this time, he's not mansplaining to me, either. It's a conversation between equals. It's . . .

Why am I being so defensive over Bradley?

Once we've sat down, I ask the question I really want to ask: "How often should I be uploading? I've done two vlogs in a week now."

"You should upload as much as you want to. There is such a thing as too much, though. I do it every week. It builds up a bit of excitement, especially if I'm featuring a specialty piece of machinery."

This conversation has gone odd. I feel like I can say anything to him, like I can with Lauren. My mouth ends up blurting out, "I've had a few people saying bad stuff. Like that I'm ugly."

Bradley brushes my arm for a millisecond and says very gently, "That is trolling, Millie. I did warn you."

And then it gets even MORE weird, so Bradley starts talking really quickly.

"But more to the point, you are funny and interesting and it's something different from the endless girl stuff. I loved your last vlog. I am so OVER girl stuff. Pinky cheeks, eyebrows, princess castles. UNICORNS WITH GOLD-TINGED MANES—WHAT IS IT ALL ABOUT?"

"You don't have to watch it, Bradley," I snap, glad to change the subject. "And a lot of girls don't like it, either, AND even if we do— AND I DO A BIT—it's not what we are all about. We can like what we like, anyway. There is no such thing as boy stuff or girl stuff! There is just STUFF!"

Bradley looks down. "Well, I've lost people I love to makeup. Like my American girlfriend. We were drifting apart, so I've decided we should probably call it a day. Better to do it before we met in real life. She was always a big cosplayer, and now she's not so into the fun side of it. I don't care about the sort of lipstick that Captain Marvel would wear. She can fly! She can shoot energy bursts from her hands! She can do hand-to-hand combat! I don't think she is going to nip into Sephora in the middle of fighting evil and ask for a consultation."

Bradley is angry. And also very funny.

"I'm sorry about your girlfriend." I have to say something.

"Well, that's the way it goes." Bradley sighs. "Long-distance stuff is always hard. Anyway, you're different. You understand that it's not just about how you look. It's BRAINS, too. BRAINS. I like brains. I like talking about stuff that's actually interesting. Not just lifts but THE WORLD. I'm a feminist, you know."

Bradley asks me really seriously, "Do you like flapjacks or cupcakes?"

This question catches me by surprise. It's not often that you go from superheroes to sponges.

"Flapjacks."

"I knew you would." Bradley does the loveliest smile a lift-loving cosplay geek vlogger could ever do. "I knew you wouldn't be taken in by all that icing. Now, you know what you should do in your next vlog? Talk about trolling and how to deal with it. Talk about how it made you feel. That's REAL. Talk about the hard stuff, Millie."

I am enjoying this afternoon far more than I thought I would. I knew I'd get a lot from it in a professional way, but I didn't expect to get into random conversations about long-distance relationships, the way people change, and cupcakes. It's all very natural and easy and . . .

#FlapjackGeekLove

That night starts with a Lauren love conspiracy theory.

"You are SO in love with Bradley Sanderson, it's not even true."

I've told her about my afternoon at the shopping center, and her response is very predictable.

"Lauren, this is going to shock you, but it *is* possible to be with a boy and not snog him. But he was lovely. He's funny. He was talking about sharks and what would happen if they got cell phones!"

Lauren stays quiet.

I try to explain a bit more. "Yes, you had to be there, but he's sweet and he looked really good. Nice jacket. A Star Wars shirt that actually he—"

Lauren interrupts, "Millie—I'm sorry, but this man is in love with you. You're so vlog-obsessed these days that you can't see the OBVIOUS that's right in front of your eyes. Well, if you don't fancy him, you should be careful not to go all Erin about him and lead him on."

This feels rather like Lauren is attacking me, so without thinking, I blurt out, "Lauren. He is NOT in love with me. He's no more in love with me than Danny is, so get that STRAIGHT out of your head!"

This is very snappy for me, and I feel nervous. Lauren and I, we don't really argue. I think we can both sense that it's getting a bit heavy. There's a pause. I'm worried about what she is going to say next. Even the thought of a fight with Lauren makes me want to throw up.

Then Lauren says, "Are you going cosplay on me? I don't mind, but if you are, can you warn me? Because if I come around here and you're dressed up like something from *The Walking Dead*, it could properly freak me out."

This makes me smile. This is classic Lauren.

"Why would I go zombie on you, Loz?"

"I don't know," she says. "I just have seriously bad zombie nightmares. HASHTAG that time my dad dressed up for Halloween and took the barbecue-sauce-over-his-head thing a bit too far. Even now, any hint of a chipotle dressing and I am seriously feeling vom. Anyway, you are now going out with a cosplayer—"

"I'm not!" I yell. "He's just my . . . media advisor!"

And we both collapse laughing at this, because clearly I am not a massive celebrity vlogger and I do not need any sort of advisor in anything.

While we giggle, Bradley direct messages me.

> Thank you for giving me your time today. Can we do it again soon? We can discuss how to stop aquatic predators with very sharp teeth getting hold of the latest technology. Imagine sharks with Tasers. B

Bradley uses the kind of words I use, and he's very clever.

Lauren asks me who's messaged me. I lie and say Gracie. I have to. It would get too complicated otherwise.

"Let's do a vlog in a bit, Loz. Why don't you stay over?"

After my time with Bradley, I'm totally fired up about doing another vlog. He's RIGHT. Focus on the followers. Tackle the trolls.

Lauren looks really pleased. "Great idea, Mills! I'll just call my mum and tell her I'll be spending the night here. To be honest, I don't think she'll notice, but you never know! Meet you in Hashtag Help Global HQ."

This is a very sweet way of describing Granddad's ever so slightly moldy shed.

#Kebab

I skip down to the shed to find Granddad is just clos-ing the door. He's carrying an old jam jar full of nails. He has lots of these. They are a bit like his pieces of wood. He never seems to use them.

He grunts at me. "Must be going well, Millie. Don't you let fame go to your head, though."

It's hardly fame, Granddad, I think, but then he still doesn't understand how to use the DVR. I'm not even going to try to begin to explain this.

"I don't understand it, Millie," Granddad continues, "but Teresa tells me it's going well. It's going better than her attempts to make a smoky-lamb-flavor ice cream, anyway."

"Do you ever get annoyed at Teresa, Granddad?" This is a sort of mean thing to ask, but I do wonder. Granddad is old-fashioned and sensible, and Teresa is . . . not.

Granddad stares at me. He looks tired. "You have to let people make their own choices, Millie. Some people think I should have been harder on my kids and then they both wouldn't be living at home with me and trying to make money in stupid ways. But there's more to life than making money and having a job that impresses people. It's called contributing, Millie. Contributing."

What does this mean? I hope I'm not going to get a gardening lecture. It was lovely of Granddad to help me out with my pumpkin competition in first grade, but I know far too much about garden plants than the average thirteen-year-old should.

"Contributing to other people's lives. Trying to make things better. There's lots of ways to do it. Picking up rubbish is a way to contribute. Just taking care of yourself is a way to contribute. Even trying to fuse a kebab and a Cornetto is a way to contribute to life. You are doing it by sharing that common sense of yours and trying to make people's lives better. I'm proud of you."

This makes me so warm inside, I could burst. Compliments from Granddad are like really rare orchids that only grow in specific climates.

I told you. I know far too much about plants.

"But just one thing, Millie." Granddad looks almost stern. "I know that brain of yours—full of ideas but full of worries, too. Don't give away so much of yourself that you've got nothing left. Don't get into situations that put you in the firing line of idiots. You're still only young. You may have an old head on those shoulders, but it's a sensitive head that needs watering, shelter, and love. Keep away from the weeds. And remember, sometimes weeds have pretty flowers."

I give him a hug.

"Now I suppose you'll be wanting my shed again. Well, you can have it. I've got a serious appointment with some begonias out front."

"Thanks, Granddad."

I love Granddad. I suppose getting trolled is as inevitable as getting your fingernails muddy when you do the gardening. You just have to toughen up and get a good liquid soap. Or something. You can't wash bad thoughts away, but you can park them in the farthest bit of the brain supermarket parking lot near the mind gas station.

I really need to get my head together before the next vlog, or no one will actually know what on earth I'm talking about.

#TrollTakedown

Lauren plods into the shed. Her eyes are a bit red. She must have been using her witch hazel wipes to redo her mascara. She squishes up her face, holds out her makeup bag, and points at me. "Now. Do you want some foundation just to make you look a bit less like actual death?"

Before I have the chance to say anything, a brush is on my face.

I very gently move Lauren's hand away. "No. Let's keep it natural and real and . . . us."

Lauren squeals. "Mills! I've just got a massive splinter from the shed."

Lauren shows me her finger. There is literally a tree sticking out of it.

"Lauren! That looks terrible! Have you had a tetanus shot? It's this disease that's in plants and wood and stuff. It makes your whole body lock up. You can't speak or anything!"

It's amazing how many things can kill you horribly. Even sweet things like blades of grass and daisies. And mushrooms. There is a type of mushroom that basically makes your liver explode. It's called a death cap. There's also a destroying angel. It sounds like something out of a horror film but it can grow in forests near your house. This is why I like living in a town. These are the sorts of things that I wish I didn't know. My head goes a bit odd and my breathing feels . . .

"So tetanus locks up your entire body? If only Erin would get it!" Lauren giggles.

This is an evil thing to say but it stops my brain spiraling down into fungus doom.

Lauren looks guilty. "Well, I don't want her to die, but it would be nice if she could shut up for a while. Though, knowing her, if she got tetanus, her face would freeze in a massive beautiful grin and she'd take a selfie from the hospital and get a million likes."

This is probably true, but I say to Lauren, "Let's just get your splinter out."

"OH!" Lauren leaps into the air. "Should will film it?! Should we do, like, a first-aid advice thing? Medical procedures get loads of views and stuff, and we—OUCH!"

It's out.

Lauren sighs, disappointed. "We really missed an opportunity there, Mills. Splinter vlogging could be massive. Do you want me to give myself another one so we can film it?"

"No, Lozza! Don't hurt yourself! Let's just do my vlog."

"Do you know what you're going to say?"

The truth is, I have a very good idea, because I haven't been thinking of much else.

"Yeah. I've got a rough idea," I mumble.

The thing is, after talking with Bradley, I now know there are people waiting to hear what I am going to say. They will get alerts when I post. Their phone will ding! Or beep! Or vibrate!

I take a deep breath. Lauren gets out of shot and sticks up her thumb.

"Hello! Millie Porter here! 'Hashtag Help Me Cope With Trolling.'"

"I'm just going to read you some of the comments that have been left on my vlog recently:

"'Talentless ugly cow. Delete your account.'

"'Why bother???? Fat and not funny.'

"'Typical woman telling us how to act. Sort your own life out.'

"'Ugliest fake ever.'"

(Reading them out loud again makes the sides of my eyes feel itchy. Got to keep bright. Got to keep sensible. I swallow.)

"It's really hard to read stuff like that, but here's what I try to remember. These people don't know me. They are just really sad, horrible people sitting in their bedrooms or at bus stops with no friends. And they probably feel dreadful and useless about themselves. If they see someone doing something fun or interesting, they just want to hurt them and bring them down.

"I'm not saying that I think you should be nice to trolls. Just ignore them, or imagine them standing in a shopping center in their underpants. That's what my mum does before big meetings, and it makes even scary people totally silly. Focus on the good stuff or the nice comments instead.

"We can all be tools. I'm not saying it's right! I'm saying inner toolness can erupt like a volcano and spew twonk magma all over your . . . shirt. Like that project I did in elementary school.

"Anyway, SERIOUSLY, bullying is horrible, and it makes your life a living misery. It could be being called names or getting slapped. It could be

to your face or online or BOTH. The point is, you shouldn't take it. Tell someone IN POWER, because you deserve to feel . . . good. No one should feel like rubbish because of other people. I KNOW that sounds preachy and dorky, but look: It is FACT. Just like it is a fact that you can't lick your elbow. Look!"

(And I try to lick my elbow.)

"And I know you're probably watching me now, thinking, 'She looks like a massive goof with no makeup,' but that just goes to show that looks can be—what's the word?—a bit wrong and um . . . just . . . just . . . don't think that you're on your own. You are NOT.

"So that's me, Millie. Hashtag Help me to help you, and leave any comments below. Unless you're a troll. You can hashtag OFF!"

It sounds good. I'm pleased. Then I hear an odd noise in the background. It's my best friend, and she is crying.

I rush over to hug her. "Lauren. What's the matter?"

Lauren sniffs. "Oh, it's just you talking about not letting other people bring you down. It makes me think of my mum and dad. I spoke to my mum, Mills, and she said I'm not allowed to stay here tonight, but you know, I honestly dread going home. What's the point of me being there? It's like when I had that piñata for my birthday and my mum started smashing it in a temper? There were Haribo gummy bears everywhere. I know that sounds sort of funny now, but it wasn't. The thing is, Mills—"

At this precise, dreadful moment for bursting in, Aunty Teresa bursts in and says, "HELLO, GIRLS!!! Oh! Lauren, are you okay? It's boys, isn't it? Don't worry, I get it. Boys do make you cry. The fact is, they do not mature till they are about twenty-three, and honestly, they are not worth crying about. Is it kissing? It's difficult, isn't it? The best thing to do is practice on your own hand. Just stick your tongue out and kind of—"

"Teresa! We don't need to hear this right now!" I yell.

Teresa actually shuts up. For four seconds.

"Okay. I'm going, but if you want to know ANYTHING about boys, just come to me. I am your woman for any information about men and ice cream. They are very similar things. Nice, but they melt under pressure. And you—"

"TERESA!" I find myself properly yelling in a way that is slightly out of control and hurts my throat. Teresa just nods her head and dashes out of the shed.

I look at Lauren. I don't really know what to say.

"Sorry!" Lauren sniffs. "It's just . . . all very hard. Anyway, listen, I'd better get home. It will only make it worse if I'm late."

I give Lauren a hug, and we go back into the house. She grabs all her stuff from my room and says a slightly teary good-bye.

I can't imagine what it must be like to go home to actual war. I know what it's like going home to total neatness and now total chaos, but THAT . . . The only really horrid stuff in my life is trolling, but at least that's the outside world. It must be horrible if your family isn't there for you. You need to look after the people you love.

My mind feels so full at the moment. There's the vlog and there's Erin and Bradley and Danny and Lauren's parents and Gary and the trolls and my head is spiraling a tiny bit. . . .

My chest feels like someone is sitting on it.

That's when I decide to call my mum.

#Mum

Mum answers the phone almost immediately. She's on Bluetooth in the car and turns down her awful music.

"Hello, darling," she says. "What's up?"

What is up? Where to start? I can't, so I say, "I just want to tell you that I love you."

Mum pauses and says, "That's good."

Then there's a massive uncomfortable silence and I find myself blurting out, "Have you had a tetanus shot lately, Mum?"

Mum sounds puzzled. "Er . . . no. The advice has changed. You only have to . . . I'm not sure. We order the needles, but I'm not a doctor, darling. If I ever start working with animals from abroad, I'll have one."

Despite working in a hospital, Mum always gets tetanus mixed up with rabies.

Mum starts to sound worried. "Millie, have you been reading about tropical diseases on Wikipedia again?"

I can't lie to my mum.

"No . . . Well, a bit. Tetanus isn't tropical, though. It's here."

"Hang on. I'm pulling over. What's really the problem, Millie? What are you worried about? I know how your head works."

And she does know. She gets me better than anyone. I just can't tell her right now.

I don't say a word, and Mum says, "Come home whenever you want. You know you can. We miss you."

It's like she is psychic.

"I know," I say to her. "Anyway, you get on. I just love you."

"I love you, too, Millie—and just before you go . . . if you ARE feeling worried about something, make a list of all the things that are on your mind. It really helps, and you can work through them one by one. It's the sensible thing to do. See you soon. Love you. Bye!"

I flop back on my bed. The truth is, I'm worried about LOTS of things. And I KNOW some of them are silly and stupid, but I can't help myself. I'm doing an advice vlog, but inside, I'm a mess.

1. My best friend may be getting tetanus.
2. My mum could possibly have tetanus, too, for all I know. She doesn't understand things she should understand—like deadly diseases.
3. I have made the worst enemy on earth in Erin.
4. I have a massive crush on a boy who will never be mine.
5. A boy who Erin really likes, too, and who really likes Erin.
6. There are really bad people on the news doing really bad things.
7. What if the bad people get hold of terrible mushrooms?

8. Okay, that one is ridiculous. Perhaps these lists do help.

9. Am I hurting my mum by not being with her?

10. Where is my dad? I thought living with him would make me feel all FREE! It just makes me feel nervous. And a bit alone.

11. Will Aunty Teresa actually kill someone with her fusion food?

12. Please let Aunty Teresa never put mushrooms in food.

13. Sometimes I worry that terrible things are happening to the people I love and there's NOTHING I can do about it.

14. People are calling me ugly, and it hurts.

15. My vlog just makes me look like a massive dork.

16. My vlog just makes me sound like a massive dork.

At that point, I get a text.

> Millie. Had a great idea about your vlog. Promise not to cosplay too much. Want to meet?

I haven't even replied to his last text. I add another point to the list.

17. I STILL don't know how I feel about Bradley.

I upload the vlog. It's 7:45 p.m. I will honestly, HONESTLY not check the vlog again till 7:00 a.m. tomorrow.

#Heart

I wake up at 4:00 a.m. on Sunday. This is just plain wrong. This time should not exist. I've had more views on the new vlog than on the previous one. I give in and check the comments.

> I watched your vlog. It's not as easy as that.

> You look fresh! I love your look! It makes a change from everyone else covered in lipstick.

> SPOON.

> Trolls aren't all tragic. Some of us genuinely hate you.

Perhaps I've taken on too much. I can't *really* tackle stuff that I haven't experienced myself, can I? I do just sound stupid and dorky. People have told me I am a total idiot, and do you know what? They are right. I better think hard about what I can vlog about next. Like Bradley says, I have to think about my brand.

But then there's one comment from @DannyTruds . . .

Another great vlog.

And a heart emoji.

A HEART!!! THAT'S EPIC.

And confusing.

Does that mean he . . . ?

Danny and Bradley are in my head a lot. Like a massive, swirl-ing boy mess. My whole body feels like a whirlwind. I need to try to go back to sleep.

#MillsTheSpills

I'm dreading school this week. I know full well that another vlog puts me right in Erin's bombing range, and I don't know how to respond to Danny's heart. It might just be a friendly heart, or it might be a big, pulsating, "LET'S BE TOGETHER" heart.

No prizes for guessing which one Lauren thinks it is. When we're searching for a table in the cafeteria at lunch, I tell her about the heart.

"He could just be being friendly," Lauren says grumpily. This isn't really the answer I want to hear. She's been grumpy all morning.

"You don't know that for sure!" I say.

"Oh, come on, Millie." Lauren almost snaps at me. "You know Danny and Erin are spending LOADS of time together. Stop being greedy! Bradley is your man! He is a major full-on nerd, and you are pretty with a mega brain. You went on a date. Do the love math."

The truth is, I think she may be right. He did look at me through his glasses in the same way that he looks at escalators—with love and respect. "But do I want to have a relationship with someone who spends all their time in lifts?"

"Lifts are sexy!" Lauren says with her big wide eyes, annoyed. "In films, people always kiss in lifts because they are private, aren't they? You could even combine vlogs! 'Hashtag Help From An Escalator.'"

This makes me laugh LOTS. "Lauren . . . don't be ridicu—"

What happens next will go down in history.

While I'm laughing, I seem to completely lose the ability to actually walk. My right leg decides it would like to break free of my body and make a dash for the other side of the room. I find myself flying through the air in slow motion. I slam my hands down to break my fall, but my tray and my food fly absolutely everywhere. I basically create a chip fountain. It's probably spectacular to watch.

The whole cafeteria erupts into clapping and cheering. This is normally what happens when someone drops their tray, but it's probably the most embarrassing thing that has ever happened to me EVER.

Lovely Gracie runs over and starts helping me pick up the chips. Lauren picks me up. She understands falling over. "It's hormonal," she whispers. "We can't help it. It causes an ankle-and-toe imbalance. Even without high heels. Remember when I did it? It's a normal part of life."

From the corner of my eye, I see Danny staring at me.

Way to go, Millie. There's nothing like a good carpet of carbohydrates when you're trying to impress the man of your dreams.

I also see Erin. The grin is wide and the phone is UP. She got all the aftermath.

Also RUNNING toward me is Bradley with another plate of

food. How did he get that so quickly? He must be sacrificing his own chips.

"Here you are, Millie!" he says. "Saves you waiting in line again."

I know where that photo is going to end up, too.

Erin has double missiles now. "The Fall" and what she would term "The Dweeb Save." She certainly doesn't approve of someone like Bradley. He's got the following, but he hasn't got any cool in her opinion.

I brush myself off and slink into a chair as fast as I can. Things get back to normal in the cafeteria quite quickly, but in my head there's a big, really bad music festival of Erin and people's mouths yelling and laughing and staring and pointing and noise and . . .

Breathe. I just have to take deep breaths and BREATHE.

"Mills, are you all right now?"

Lauren knows that the answer to this question is no, but she isn't sure what to do about it. Her asking "Are you all right?" is kind of her way of saying "Please be okay" and "I don't know what to do to make you feel better."

I tell her I'm fine, but my heart is racing and I feel dizzy and sick and like I might explode. Of course I'm not fine. What just happened is embarrassing in a terminal way.

When he's actually around, my dad *still* talks about things that happened to people at school, and he's ancient. He can't remember his credit card PIN, but he can tell you about the time Nicholas Clarkson's swimming trunks floated to the top of the swimming pool before Nicholas Clarkson did. He was called "Nudey Nick" for SEVEN years after that. My dad still calls him it. To my dad, he'll *always* be "NUDEY NICK, NUDEY NICK, YOUR BARE

BOTTOM MAKES US SICK." They even made up a song for him.

Now I'll be Mills . . . MILLS THE SPILLS. It even rhymes! "Mills the Spills, Mills the Spills, with her dropped-chip-lunch coolness, she kills." I will be called this forever. Even when I am forty-three and living in—

Breathe, Millie. Breathe. That's what I have to say to myself.

It's at times like this that my mum rushes into my head and says, *"Millie, you're fine. You're okay. You're okay."* It's like she's chanting it. She's done it in real life, and she does it in my brain when I need her to.

Eventually, I sense the feeling come back to my face a bit. My second lunch has gone very cold, and I just push it away. I feel bad rejecting Bradley's chips, but I've lost my appetite completely. My mouth isn't working, but my eyes are. Erin has squeezed next to Danny, and they are giggling. I know what will happen now. . . .

#EnjoyYourTrip

Later on, as we're walking home from school, Lauren checks her phone.

"You're on Mr. Style Shame, Mills. But that was pretty inevitable, really. Anyone in the cafeteria could have sent him that photo. And it's not got THAT many likes."

I don't really know how I feel about this. "Check Erin's account, Loz."

"Millie! She's got over nine thousand followers now. And there are loads of photos of her and Danny. They do look really good together."

This feels a bit much. I death-stare Lauren. "I know. I've seen them."

"Oh! She's also posted a photo of all your spilled chips and the smashed plate! But the caption is actually really nice. Look! Why would she do that?"

I read what Erin has written.

Don't you just love that feeling you get when you see two people who are just meant to be together? Today

at school a girl fell over and dropped her lunch tray,
and a lovely boy helped her up #ChipRomance
#GeekLove I heart seeing people who might not be
lucky enough to have loads of friends being kind to
other people who really do need #Help #Heartwarming

"You see," Lauren says. "That's actually really lovely."

Lauren has completely missed the evil point. "So it's kind to say someone really needs help and is less fortunate than you?"

"I've heard you say things sort of like that," Lauren snaps back.

And Lauren has, but this is different. Erin is a genius of horrible. She can make it sound nice, but I know this is just a really clever way to have a dig at me. I know I'm right because underneath people have commented with a whole load of crying-with-laughter emojis and *TRAGIC!*s. But there's no way to respond—if I have a go at her, it's ME who looks like a cow.

Lauren can see that I'm flat, but she's acting all hard and odd. "Why don't you vlog about how falling over isn't the worst thing in the world, even though, at the moment, it feels like that. You do need to get over yourself a bit, Mills. It really could have been worse."

Lauren has completely failed to grasp that I am having a total life disaster. All I can think of and all I can hear is the amount of people who are either laughing at me or feeling sorry for me all over the world.

"Bye, Millie. Hope you feel better."

You'd think your BFF would be able to make you feel better. But Lauren just slinks off into the sunlight.

When I get back to Granddad's, I slam my bag on the sofa and sort of collapse like a massive splat of pasta sauce that's jumped off Teresa's plate. She's the world's messiest eater.

UNBELIEVABLY, Dad is home AND he actually notices that I am down. "What's up, Lady Mills?"

He says it like he thinks it's something minor. He's missed out on loads. There's no point telling him about what Erin has done. He won't get it and will just say something sweet but useless. So I tell him that I fell over in the cafeteria and my chips went everywhere.

Dad doesn't laugh or say I'm being stupid. He just says, "You must have felt very embarrassed by that."

Which I did and I do, but, in a way, I want him to say, "Don't be silly, Millie! It's just a fall," or "Pick yourself up and get on with it!" like Mum would. But Dad is not Mum. He is sweet in a different way. In an understanding way. I can't believe I do not want understanding. What is happening to me?!

But now that I've got Dad, I might as well talk to him.

"It's just that I remember you telling me about Nicholas Clarkson, Dad, and the time he lost his trunks—and that was twenty years ago. Even I can sing the song about him—"

Dad interrupts me. "Yes, I did tease him, Millie. But do you know what Nicholas Clarkson is doing now? He develops apps and software, drives a Porsche, and goes to Barbados twice a year. I think he's got over the fact that he was naked in a swimming pool decades ago. He probably swims naked out of choice in his own private swimming pool now. No one is laughing at him. He's laughing at us. Life is a marathon, Mills—not a sprint. And in the marathon, he's at the finish line getting his medal and bar of chocolate, and I'm at mile two with a stitch in my side. I'm racing around trying to make money. I'm missing out on you growing up, even though you're here. I'm making a mess of it all, Millie. . . ."

Dad looks gutted. The thing is, he is sort of right; he still lives with his dad and sister and I haven't seen him for quite a long time. But then I remember what Granddad told me: Dad's funny and kind. He's sweet to me. He still gets on with Mum.

"You're not making a mess of things. I think you're brilliant," I say, and I give him a hug.

Dad has brought out my sensible, problem-sorter side again. I feel better.

"Oh, ignore your old dad. You make things very excellent being here, and I'm very proud of you. You won't end up like me. You, Millie, have BRAINS. Your dad's handsome looks"—and he winks—"but your mother's brain. If I were you, I would just forget about tripping. It's a momentary lapse in a life that is otherwise fairly glorious, wouldn't you say?"

Dad pats me on the back and says, "Right, lady. What would you like for tea? Chips? CHIPS! CHIPS! Let's have chips, Millie. Let's reestablish chips as lovely things in your mind. LET US REHABILITATE THE MIGHTY CHIP-O AND REMIND YOU THAT FRIED FOOD IS YOUR FRIEND!"

Dad shouting brings Granddad in. "What on earth is going on?" he grumbles. "Why are we shouting about chips? Is that what it's come to? Excitement about potatoes?"

Dad laughs and starts dancing around Granddad. "Yes! Yes! It has. Chips! Chips! FRIED BROWN CRISPY LOVELY CHIIIIIPSSSSSS!"

"Daft fool!" Granddad eventually says. This makes both Dad and me giggle a lot.

I feel better and brave again.

"Can I borrow your shed, Granddad?"

"Well, I was going to escape from this house of nutters to do some potting, but go on then. I can't be saved from them, but perhaps you can."

Dad's chat has left me feeling a bit better. Why do these little things matter? They shouldn't. It's like everything gets completely blown out of proportion. And I want to tell everyone that they shouldn't and that you can lose your pants and still end up having amazing foreign holidays. I won't say that, but I will tell people that TINY MISTAKES JUST DON'T MATTER. And Erin and her brilliant frayed-in-just-the-right-places jeans and her totally amazing way of being horrible while pretending to be nice can just go and CRASH in an I've-lost-my-Wi-Fi-and-nothing-is-downloading way.

I don't want her to actually crash.

#KeepingItReal

I position the camera. I'm ready to share. I don't even message Lauren. She obviously doesn't care that much. I just do it.

"*Hello. Millie Porter—back sooner than I thought. Thanks for all your comments. Well—thanks for the nice ones. The other ones—whatever.*

"*Today: 'Hashtag Help Me Cope With Social Death'—those times when something horrible happens in front of everyone. Let me tell you what happened today. If you go to my school, you know already.*

"*Basically, I'd just collected my lunch from Mary the cafeteria lady, and she has amazing dreads. Anyway, I was looking at her purple tips and pink roots and talking to my BFF Lauren and then I fell over my own feet and made a chip carpet. Which was embarrassing beyond belief. Can I just officially thank Lauren and the totally cool Gracie, who picked me up and didn't just stand there and stare or laugh or clap or whatever. Gracie—you have the best eye makeup ever and you are also actually a lovely person. Thank you. Also Bradley—thanks for the replacement food.*

"*Anyway. The aftermath of my fall is being shared around, and that's pretty terrible. And you know what? I'm gutted, but . . .*

"*No. I'm gutted.*

"*And I was going to hide away from it. But then I thought, 'All I have done is drop some chips. SO WHAT?! WHO CARES?!'*"

I start to get mad here.

"*IT WAS SOME CHIPS ON A FLOOR. If a seagull had been in the school cafeteria, he would have been epically happy. I am SICK of feeling like my every move is being watched by people who cannot wait for me to go wrong. So this is ME, Millie, saying NOW—THESE PEOPLE, LIKE MR. STYLE SHAME, WHO CALL PEOPLE OUT ON INSTAGRAM should be IGNORED. Stop giving them attention. Falls are not that big a deal. NOR ARE LIFE FAILS. Really. And to prove that, I am going to fall over again.*"

(And I do. Badly. Spoon. But it makes my point.)

"*No, there were no chips with that one, but you get it.*

"*But I just want to say to you: If that happens to you, you don't need to hide away. You don't need to feel embarrassed or ashamed. You fell over. You dropped some chips. You did WHATEVER. You did not in any way hurt anyone. If you get caught doing something that makes you feel stupid, SO WHAT?! DROPPING YOUR LUNCH IS NORMAL. And you shouldn't have to feel bad about it.*

"*And another thing—photos of people eating. No one looks glamorous when they are eating. I have here a sandwich made by my aunty Teresa. It has cheese, and I am going to eat it.*

"*Do what you like. Do NOT BE SHAMED. This is Millie. Hashtag Help me to help you. Thank you. Good night—and don't feel bad about yourself!*"

(And I take a massive bite of this sandwich and stop filming.)

Honestly, I don't feel very comfortable with how I look on-screen, either. Even though I am real on my vlog, I'm not totally real. You can't share ALL of you. Like Granddad says, there'd be nothing left.

If I'm honest, it's not the same without Lauren. It's not as much fun, and without her, it's not as good. She's like my cheerleader.

I message her, telling her I've uploaded a new one. I can see that she's read it, but I get nothing back. What is wrong with her?! She sits on her phone. It's never out of her hand. It's—

MUM.

Oh, CHUFFING CHUFF.

She's shouting my name from outside. Why is she here? I must be in trouble again. There's no way she'd be around here at this time if I'm not.

#AngryMum

Dad is hiding. He's stopped singing about chips because he can still read Mum's moods very well and she's not in a good one. He peeks out from behind the door in the hallway and pretends to cut his neck with his hand. This is our code for *She is ready to kill someone.*

Aunty Teresa has decided the ice-cream van needs urgent maintenance (to be fair, it does and always will). Even Granddad has run to the shed. And he used to be a Royal Marine who lived on insect omelets in the jungle and did twenty-mile runs with fourteen bricks in his rucksack. Or something.

Mum is terrifying. Magnificent but terrifying. Which is great when you're seven and your teacher makes you a tree in the Christmas play rather than a shepherd because he thinks "that's a job for boys." It's great when your mum storms up to the school to complain and, the next thing you know, you're carrying a shepherd hook and Kyle Turner is being your sheep. That was fantastic, but it's not so good now.

Mum does her quiet psycho voice. She doesn't lose her temper. She is reasonable. Apart from the time she threw a hand blender across the kitchen, she has always been a model of total control. Zero spoon and maximum excellence.

She stares at me.

"Millie, we need to talk. I'm worried that you are giving away too much about your life online. Why do you want to share it all with strangers? Why can't you talk to me about all this? That's what I'm here for!"

"Mum!" I feel very like I know what I'm doing here. "I don't want to fall out with you about it, but the whole point is that my vlog is about being honest. I wanted to do something different, and that means being REAL and—"

"Can I stop you there?" she interrupts. "Have you considered, Millie, the implications of what you are doing? Millie, I know you are very emotionally intelligent FOR YOUR AGE and always have been. I'm not going to patronize you. And I'm proud of you for try-ing to help people. But I'm your mother, and it's my job to keep you safe and well. I've read the comments people have left and they are horrible. Horrible. And when I think of my little girl having to read that from . . . well, I don't know what those people are, but I don't want you anywhere near them, Millie. And don't tell me you're not affected by it, because I know you are."

And I am affected. I really am. Who wouldn't be? It's awful.

Mum looks like she's about to sob massively. "You're my little girl."

This is my chance to explain. "Mum. You told me I should never stop what I want to do because other people might laugh at me. You have always stuck up for me. That's why I became a shepherd and not a tree. Now I can fight trolls!"

172

"But you shouldn't have to!" Mum REALLY YELLS. "I nearly joined YouTube myself. I was going to call myself 'MilliesMum' and have a go at all the tools that said nasty things to you. You're very good, Millie. You present well, and you're funny. And no, you don't need makeup. You can use it if you want to, but you don't need it. Come off YouTube, Millie. Please."

"I can handle it!" I yell.

"Can you really, Millie?" Mum whispers.

I look at Mum and start to cry. It just all hits me. The names. The "ugly" thing. The fountain of chips. Danny seeing me create a fountain of chips. Lauren being all cold and weird.

"See!" Mum hugs me. "This wouldn't have happened if you were still living with me."

"Oh, Mum!" That just makes me cross. "Nothing would have happened if I still lived with you because I had to do everything your way. It wasn't all Gary and McWhirter's fault. It's you, too! Even though I never did anything stupid, you always had to tell me what I should or shouldn't be doing."

This isn't fair AT ALL, but I'm not feeling fair.

Mum sighs. "Perhaps I was a bit tough on you, but I'm so proud of what I've created. It's a tough world, Millie! VERY tough. Just give the vlogging a rest for a little while. That will be the sensible thing to do."

I can't believe I'm saying this, but I agree. "Okay, I'll THINK about it."

Mum hugs me again and says, "Thank you."

She leaves, and Dad comes out of hiding.

When I'm back in my bedroom, I've got a message from Danny.

> Sorry about the chips. The great news is, you fall over
> really well. Can't wait to see how you tackle exploding
> food in your vlog ☺

I don't think Danny is being horrible! He's trying to make me smile. Like REAL friends do.

I message him.

> I'm giving up #Help ☹

He responds immediately.

> Why? Are you going to make a big announcement
> about it?

> The trolls and stuff . . . No. I haven't decided what to
> do yet.

> Millie, don't do this because of dumb comments.
> You do know you're not ugly, don't you? Red-lipped
> batfish—they are ugly. But not you.

> What's a red-lipped batfish?

I'm almost frightened to ask.

> It's this fish that looks like it has put red lipstick on in
> the dark and has a lamp on its head. It could never do

a vlog. I saw it on Animal Planet. Dad was building a
naval destroyer and there was nothing else on.

He sends me a photo of it.

I act cool. I don't know how to respond. So I don't. Why is Danny
telling me I am not ugly? This feels weird.

My phone dings. Just when I thought my life couldn't get any
worse, I have a notification. Erin Breeler's new vlog has launched.
Of course I have to see it.

#Kittens

Erin Breeler is wearing kitten ears. Even for a Monday, this is a new low.

She looks phenomenal on camera. The bedroom behind her has been lit perfectly. Her duvet has this Moroccan pattern with a matching lamp. Her dressing table is covered in cards and photos. It's all so professional and perfect. She tilts her head in the classic Erin way and starts speaking.

"Hi! Do you like my ears? So, basically, a whole load of you have been saying, 'Erin, PLEASE do a vlog. Please.' And yeah. Okay. With pleasure. And this is going to be about makeup and fashion and styling because . . . that's what I do. I think when you come on here, you want to get away from all the awful stuff that's going on in your life. You don't want to be thinking about solving problems and how to deal with social embarrassment. This is all about looking good and feeling good and NOT—"

(And she laughs this really annoyingly sweet but EVIL laugh.)

"—about how you recover from falling over. . . ."

I turn it off.

I just don't want to watch any more.

But I can't stop myself looking. I turn it back on.

Erin demonstrates different ways to wrap a scarf so it can be a sarong, a top, a headscarf, and a skirt. She also shows how you can tie it to make a bag. THEN she gets a pair of thick tights and shares her secrets to the perfect rip.

It's an epic watch.

Erin's latest vlog is a fashion triumph.

My latest vlog is about dropping your lunch.

Already, she has had almost the same number of views as my cat vlog.

I think a break from vlogging is a very good idea indeed. I would also like a break from other people. Dave snuggles beside me. She may be wild, but she understands a bad mood created by a good vlog better than any human ever could.

#WrappedUp

The next day at school, Lauren isn't around. Maybe she's ill. It must be why she hasn't replied to my messages.

I'm on my own, so I try to do a Bradley and hug the walls. And I don't go anywhere near chips. I opt for a nice vegetarian wrap, as, even if you do drop it, the cheese, peppers, and avocado are all contained. There won't be a food bomb. I'm just about to bite into it when someone sits beside me.

I assume it's lovely Gracie, so I say, "Wanna bite?"

A very Canadian voice answers, "Er . . . no, thank you—but thanks for asking."

I nearly choke. Danny Trudeau is sitting next to me.

"Ah, gone for the safe option today. The sturdy wrap. If it falls, it falls as ONE."

My mouth and brain sort of refuse to work together. I just stare.

Danny carries on. "I was thinking about what you said last night. I like Hashtag Help, and I don't want you to stop vlogging. It's . . . interesting. It's something new, and it's different. I get kinda bored with all the makeup stuff or the wacky prankster vloggers. I think it's great that you're so real."

(This is just what Bradley said—he was RIGHT!)

"It's sweet to want to help people out. It's a hard world. It's nice to watch something that makes you laugh—especially after moving here and not knowing anyone. You know, I think the dinosaurs died out because they had no Internet or TV and died of boredom."

"Really?" This is the only word I manage to say. I must look really confused.

"Yeah." Danny smiles. "Just think, at the end of a hard day chasing stuff, you just want to get back to your cave and watch something."

At first, I don't laugh, because I don't really get it. Then I remember—that vlog where I said that dinosaurs died out because they didn't embrace feminism.

"Oh. Yeah." I'm in a panic. "They needed a show featuring a really glamorous family of brontosauruses. They could call it *Keeping Up with the Jurassics* or something."

This isn't meant to be a brilliantly hilarious joke, but Danny tilts his head back and howls like a maniac. He laughs so loud that basically everyone who wasn't looking before is now looking.

Including Erin. She's staring at us HARD.

Oh, please don't talk to me when she's watching.

"Anyway." Danny interrupts my head panic. "I just wanted to tell you that. It's neat. You're neat. And I like what you said about falling over not being the end of the world. It's not. It's just falling over. Life is falling over, you know, and getting back up again."

So he's not just good-looking; he's sensible, too. And a philosopher. I want to snog him immediately. Like now. But instead, I say, "Thanks, Danny. That's . . . good."

I can't really concentrate because now BRADLEY is walking up to my table, looking very grumpy.

Danny quickly leaves, and Bradley sits down. "Are you two going out?"

"No!" I sort of half yell and half whisper. "He just wanted to tell me I was . . . neat."

"Good!" Bradley snaps. I stare at him.

Bradley notices. "Well, I don't think you'd enjoy going out with a Canadian. He'll probably fly back there soon, and I know from my lift contacts that Canadians are very . . . different. They probably hide behind all those maple leaves and do their dating in forests."

I think this is Bradley trying to be funny. It's not really.

"Bradley, he was only being nice. He's interested in the vlog. Right, I've just got to go and ask Gracie where she gets her mascara from. It wouldn't run in a monsoon. It's EPIC!"

I know any makeup talk will send Bradley away kindly. And it does.

I leave the cafeteria. As I turn the corner to the main block of the school, my path is blocked. What blocks me is solid, tall, and very scary. Glossy lips shine like very dangerous Olympic ski slopes, and teeth as white as gourmet ice cream frozen with liquid nitrogen gleam at me.

It's Erin.

"Millie Porter," she says. "It's time you and I had a . . . talk."

#Showdown

Erin does her beautiful head tilt and snarls. She's whispering, but to me, her message is loud and clear.

"You think you're cool. You're not."

I go all pathetic. "I don't think I'm cool at all."

"Yes, you do," she whispers. "But YOU are small. My vlog has already had thousands of views. No one wants to see you giving us your advice. Who do you think you are?"

This makes me angry, and I have an attack of the braves.

"I've had loads of views, too. And I know you've looked at my vlogs because of your Instagram. And I think you've been doing some enormous trolling."

Erin tilts her head to the other, equally glamorous, side. We should ALL be over girl-on-girl hate, but Erin makes it impossible.

"The trolling is nothing to do with me," she growls. "I don't mind telling you what I think of you to your face. Do you know what people say about you behind your back? That you're DULLSVILLE! That you think not wearing makeup is a new thing that makes you some kind of amazing rebel. You are not going to change the world and get a prize, Millie. It's all been done. And people are doing it BETTER."

I start to lose it now. "I KNOW. All I'm trying to do is help people because I'm dull and sensible, Erin! And because being around you has totally taught me how to deal with twonks who only love themselves and want to make other people's lives a misery."

And then Erin goes all Disney evil queen and says, "I can destroy you. Never forget it. Leave this to the people who actually know what they are doing and have something to say. Leave Instagramming to people who want to make this world look better, not worse. Basically, Millie BORING Porter—WIND IT IN, GET LOST, and DISAPPEAR!"

She still isn't finished, though.

"Oh, and don't for one second think that Danny is interested in you. We are going bowling after school this week. That was a pity chat. He's a nice boy, and he feels SORRY for you. He's not attracted to you. Boys like him would never go out with girls like you. This isn't a cute fairy-tale land where the gorgeous boy likes the clever girl. Go and have your happy ending with the lift geek. You can spend your time pressing buttons and misusing the emergency bell. Thrilling!"

Then Erin Breeler glides off.

My mind tries to find lots of amazing things to say. I reach right into my brain, but I've got nothing. So I stand there like the goldfish Dave brought in from someone's pond once. All tragic and flapping and gasping for air. Erin has played with me like Dave played

with that fish, and now she's dumped me in the kitchen by the microwave, expecting someone else to clean me up.

I'm destroyed.

I'm having a full-on attack.

I need to get away NOW.

#Escape

I rush to the Zen Loo. My heart is pumping like it would if I'd been in a situation of extreme terror. I've googled this. It's very unlikely that I will die from this Erin attack—it just feels like it at the moment. I splash water on my face and breathe in deep breaths. And then I go into a cubicle and cry and cry till my face probably looks like a red-lipped batfish.

WHERE IS LAUREN WHEN I NEED HER?! Trust her to have the flu when I'm having a minor meltdown.

When I leave, Bradley is waiting for me AGAIN. "Do you need more toilet paper, Millie?"

"No, I'm okay," I sniff. "How did you know I was here?"

"I guessed," Bradley whispers. "The whole school is talking about it. There's a photo of you and Erin. It was a Snapchat, but it's been screengrabbed. I think she probably had someone waiting to take it. It was a planned attack. An ambush."

"Is it bad?" I don't really want to know the answer.

"No, it just looks like you're talking."

"We weren't. She went for me."

"Of course she did, Millie! You are totally being successful by just being you, and you're getting attention. Sometimes getting bombed is a sign of success!"

I sniff. I can't stop crying.

"I think I'm the stupidest person in the world. I don't feel wise anymore."

Bradley smiles at me and gives me a big hug. It's surprisingly nice being hugged by Bradley. "No, you're not stupid. I've had my trousers on inside out for two hours today. Everyone knows my mum shops at Tesco now and that I am size fifteen."

This makes me smile a bit. It reminds me of the sort of thing Lauren would say. Lozza is a queen. And she is sweet and funny and kind and her occasional toolness only hurts her. Never anyone else. Except that time with the squirrel. And we don't talk about that.

Why hasn't she messaged me? I MISS HER.

"Come on, Millie," Bradley says. "Don't let her see that she's made you feel bad."

I look up at him blearily. "What I really need now is some cucumber. Not to scare cats with—but to put on my eyes to reduce inflammation. Or tea bags. They tend to be more common than cucumbers in schools and in life, generally."

And then something comes over me. Rushing and real. Confused but all certain at the same crashing time. I kiss Bradley Sanderson hard on the lips. And just as he puts his arms around me, I pull back.

Bradley has gone bright red but seems quite pleased.

"OR," I quickly continue, "I should wear my enormously glam and exceedingly slightly ludicrous sunglasses ALL day. Though that will make me look like I'm hiding after a scandal."

Bradley pauses. "Well, um—you are, really, Millie."

Bradley is right. This is what everyone will be talking about for months. The day that Erin completely took down Millie Porter. It will become legend. I bet Erin is already planning the statue that will go on the spot. I will forever be cast in bronze as—

Okay, my head is probably going a bit overboard there. But still. This is big.

And why did I kiss Bradley Sanderson?

#Twisted

"You can't be beaten by her!"

At the end of school, I call Aunty Teresa and tell her everything—apart from Bradley.

"Do you want me to have a word with her, Mills?"

I have a vision of Aunty Teresa turning up to school in her ice-cream van and shoving a giant Cornetto in Erin's FACE. It's a lovely fantasy that I may think about for days.

Gracie comes up to me mid–Aunty Teresa's anti-Erin ranting and makes a motion that I need to get off the phone FAST.

"Millie. I don't know how to break this to you, AND PLEASE DON'T TELL ANYONE I TOLD YOU, but . . . Erin is telling everyone that you were having a go at her. The Snapchat shows you and her arguing. The fact is, you look very cross, like you're the one who is laying into her and telling her to back off. Look!"

Sure enough, when I see them, what I thought was my blank expression of spoon actually seems like a death stare. Bradley was COMPLETELY wrong when he said it looked like we were just talking. I'm like a cheetah eyeing up a gazelle before getting it by the neck and ripping it to pieces, then eating it in front of a really excited cameraman.

"It does look a bit . . . bad."

I can't believe how she can twist things.

"What can I do about it?"

Gracie goes very quiet and then says, "Nothing, Millie. You can't fight that. You can't beat her. She's amazing." Gracie realizes what she's said. "Horrible, don't get me wrong, but amazing."

I look over to the edge of the mobile classrooms that were meant to be temporary but have been there since Roman times and see a crowd of girls comforting Erin. She shakes her head and wipes her eyes, but when she catches me looking at her, she flashes a perfect grin. There are already sharks with cameras walking around, menacing people. I've seen them. They are called Erin. That's what I would have told Bradley. If I hadn't kissed him.

#Revenge

At home, things seem a bit better. Teresa and Dad are
doing a dance routine to an old song called "Groove Is in the Heart."
Granddad is tutting and shaking his head but looking impressed at
the same time.

Dave is sleeping on top of a perfectly ironed pile of washing.
She's shedding, and she's created a new teensy, tabby hair sweater
on top of a pair of granddad's pants. He'll be so mad when he sees
them, so I take Dave to the back garden for a brush. Dave purrs
and rolls with pleasure, then bites me when she's had enough. If
humans treated their hairdressers this way, they would be sent to
prison.

When I get back inside, there's a message from Gracie on my
phone.

Millie. Don't get freaked out again

(This means there's totally something to get freaked out about.)

But take a look at Erin's Instagram

My heart goes in my mouth. There's a beautiful black-and-white photo of Erin looking sad. What is it about black and white? It makes anything artistic and serious. Even Dave the girl-cat-thug would look artistic with that filter. Erin has hashtagged it #Sad, #Leaving, and #Unhappy and has written:

> So anyway I've been really struggling with some of the things that have been said to me on here and in person today. Someone attacked me today and said that I should leave all this to the people who do it better. Look at me. It hurt. IT HURTS.
>
> I know people are aiming stuff at me and it's just too much so I am going to come off social media for a time. I think that way I can just get my head together. And that means my vlog, too. I only ever started it as a bit of fun and I do not deserve the abuse I am getting from certain people. Plus I have to tell you that I need to concentrate on my personal life a bit more. I know lots of you are going to be very disappointed by this but the truth is everyone has their limits and I have reached mine. Love you. Erin x

I cannot believe people are falling for Erin's total "I am a victim" nonsense. All the things SHE said to me, she is now saying that I said to HER. I didn't. I wouldn't. That's just not me. I wish it was. But it's NOT.

The comments that have already been left are unbelievable:

Don't let the haters get you down.

Name and shame the bullies here. I will personally go after them.

After my dog died your Instagram page was the one thing that made me smile again. You bring joy to millions. Don't stop.

That is totally her making up her own comments.

I ring Lauren. There's still no answer.

I can't believe Erin is making me out to be completely evil and horrible when SHE is the one who is causing all the problems! SHE is the one who is having a go at me, and now she is making out that she is the victim. Some people might actually believe that I'm like that, and YES, I do mean Danny.

Danny.

Danny would want me to do a vlog now. Wouldn't he?

So would Bradley.

I'm going to do a vlog. It doesn't have to be aimed at Erin. It can just be about how people can say what they like about you on social media and that you've got no control over that.

I've got to say something.

#Catastrophe

In Granddad's shed, it's just Dave and me. Everyone in the house is either dancing or pretending to not enjoy dancing, so this is the best place to be.

I don't feel like vlogging, but I do.

"Hello. Millie here, and I'm feeling a bit rubbish."

(At this point Dave jumps on my lap. I think she feels bad about biting me after I'd made her look good.)

" 'Hashtag Help Me Cope When People Say Bad Things About Me Which Are Clearly NOT TRUE.'

"So Dave and I are just sitting here, and I've just been wondering about all this and what you might think about what I'm doing on here. The thing is, I can't bear the thought of anyone hating me. I make out that I don't care, but I do. And it's the hardest thing, because I really like people to like me. God, that sounds PATHETIC. I'm aware of that, but I do."

(I look at Dave. It's random, but I have an idea.)

"This is Dave, my cat. She's a girl, but she's called Dave. You might have seen her in some of my other vlogs. Anyway, Dave doesn't really care about anyone and what anyone thinks. She does what she likes. And yes— she's a cat, but I think there's a lot to be learned from her attitude. I know

people who HATE Dave and think she's a walking fur menace, er . . . a bag of fleas, a pit bull in a cat body—people say all sorts of things about her, and she just carries on doing her thing.

"And that's kind of what I want to say. I get people asking me about what to do when people say horrible or untrue things on the Internet. And something has happened to me this week—I know someone was having a go at me and basically making me out to be a Queen of Evil when actually THEY were the person who was . . . just being nasty and, oh . . . hugely a twonk. And some people believe that I'm like that because they want to believe it. There's nothing I can do about that. I just have to know that the people who really know me know what I'm really like, and they are the ones who matter.

"The thing is, it still hurts. It REALLY DOES, but I look at Dave and I think about that time that my mum's next-door neighbor called her the worst cat on earth and accused her of getting her pedigree cat pregnant till she found out Dave was actually a girl and not a lesbian, either. Dave just took the abuse and carried on using their cat flap to steal food. We've all just got to keep on being ourselves and ignoring the haters, and, as I always say, please tell someone. I know. I KNOW! Boring advice. Dullsville central, but seriously, it will be okay if you just talk to people you love and trust and um . . . yep. That's it from me. Be more like Dave."

(And at that point Dave attacks the phone because she feels like it. So I add—)

"But don't attack phones or sit on freshly washed trousers and shed your hair. Also if you wake me up at five o'clock in the morning by punching my face because you want food, you won't be popular.

"Thanks again. Millie out. Hashtag Help me to help you, even though today I think I need help more than anyone."

This says everything I want it to, even though it suggests humans should be more like scabby, slightly insane cats.

I'm uploading it, though. At least it's me doing something.

I give Dave a special hug. She may be full of fleas, but she really is an icon for modern women. And cats. And probably even dogs if they would just listen.

#BFFRescue

The next day Lauren is home sick. AGAIN. She normally likes Wednesdays, too. And as I have to avoid both Danny and Bradley, the day goes really slowly. I get to check the comments on my vlog once. They are mainly about Dave.

> Dave, tho.

> Cat BAE.

> Both need thereapy

(Spell *therapy* right if you are going to suggest it!)

> Nothing wrong with lesbian cats. Love is love.

I feel like replying, "I am totally for marriage equality." Then I realize that cats can't get married anyway. Or perhaps they do and just don't invite us.

When I get home, I find Aunty Teresa dressed in Victorian clothes and talking to herself.

"And they say that if you come here at night, you will see the ghost of a man who drowned after tending an injured duck. If you close your eyes tightly, you will hear his gentle quacking. Oh, hello, Millie!" she says when she spots me. "I'm just practicing! Your dad and I are doing a ghost tour."

"I didn't know there were any ghosts around here." I'm used to being confused by Teresa, but this is totally bizarre.

"Oh, there's not!" Aunty Teresa says casually. "We're just going to make them up."

"You can't do that!" I shout. "That must be illegal."

"Yes, we can, Millie. Someone made it all up once. Why not us? We will live in legend. WE WILL CREATE LEGEND!" Teresa roars.

Dad thunders into the room dressed as a ghost. He asks Teresa, "Is this going to work?"

I answer for her. "No, Dad—it's not. You don't look like a ghost. You look like a sheet."

"Actually, clever clogs," Dad says, "I'm a Roman. This is a toga. I'm the ghost of Emperor Caesar!"

This is too much. "Dad! Emperor Caesar never lived around here. That's just a load of . . ."

Teresa gets quite aggressive. "You cannot prove, Millie, that Caesar did not come here on holiday. And, anyway, there were lots of Caesars. We need to do ghosts of all historical eras."

"There was only one Caesar around here," I say, "and he was actually a salad."

When Teresa and Dad are like this, there's only one place to go: away.

I sit in my room and think about Lauren. This is the longest we haven't spoken. And she wasn't even away from school this long when she had conjunctivitis. I check all her accounts. She's posted a photo of a rainbow meme on Instagram with some ridiculous message about how "There can be no rainbow without a storm."

So she can't look after me in my hour of total need, but she's well enough to make other people feel good. I feel a bit . . . rejected.

I check my views. There are a few more but no new subscribers. And all the new comments are about Dave.

Gonna change my name to Dave. TRIBUTE.

More Le Chat. Less Chat.

I hate it when people try to be clever and funny and they are NEITHER. It's just annoying.

Dear Brain,

Think about something that makes you feel good. NOT Bradley. Think about Danny. Please don't let Erin's post have made him think I'm a cow.

I catch up on Canada, which I know a bit about. We have the same queen, but they have better ice cream and it's bigger. Also there are more things that can kill you in Canada, like snakes, spiders, and the West Nile virus, which makes your brain basically explode. And if that doesn't get you, then the bears will, and the only way to stop them attacking is to pretend you are dead already and hope the bear is a stupid one.

I take a deep breath. I imagine what would happen if Danny and I ever became a "thing." I would probably say we should live here. I can't do bears. Or elk. They charge during the mating season. I don't even want to watch things with antlers kissing. Don't charge at me for accidentally stumbling on your love thing like a spoon. I didn't mean to. It was an accident! Carry on kissing your moosey girlfriend.

Why am I talking to an imaginary elk?

You know why. Love makes you do crazy things.

Teresa walks into my bedroom.

"Sorry. Don't mind me," she tries to whisper. "We just need more paranormal props for the ghost tour. Does this Barbie seem spooky to you?"

I look at her. "She's got one arm, so I suppose so."

"Yeah," Aunty Teresa agrees. "I'm going to say it was a voodoo doll that was used in a ritualistic murder that happened in this house."

"There WILL be a murder here in a minute if someone doesn't come and tidy up this front room," Granddad yells from the bottom of the stairs.

"Be honest, Mills. What's more disturbing: a one-armed Barbie, or a Furby with a pulled-out eye?"

"Why don't you use them both?" I suggest. "You could call them a duo of death."

"Millie!" Aunty Teresa rushes over and hugs me. "Every so often I sense that you have a spark of our entrepreneurial spirit, our joie de vivre, our—"

Now Granddad bursts in. Why is there no privacy in this house?

"You're being ruddy crackers. Don't get involved, Millie. Never mind ghosts; these two will put me in an early grave."

Granddad looks at me. "And will you be requiring my shed today for one of your things that you do for your friends on the phone?"

I say "no" without letting my entire face say *I AM HIDING AWAY FROM THE ENTIRE WORLD.*

Granddad just shuffles off. Sometimes I am tremendous at pretending things are okay when they are clearly NOT.

Five minutes later, when I am still feeling quite excellent about fooling Granddad, Mum texts me. She still texts. Even though it costs money. She says she doesn't trust the other things.

Anything you'd like to tell me, Millie?

I reply.

No. Why? Love you x

She replies instantly.

**No reason. No problem. I'm here if you need me.
Love you. XX**

I think Mum has got a mind-melding machine in her head and she knows everything that goes on in my brain. Which is a worry. For both of us.

I just realized that mind melds are what they do in *Star Trek*. Sometimes it scares me how deep Bradley has got into my head. He's there all the time like a small glowing lift, going up and down the floors of my brain. Never stopping. Just up and down. Waiting for me to get on and get in touch with him.

Which I still haven't done since I kissed him.

And then I realize that makes me sound like the most full-of-myself, love-yourself horror girl since Erin Breeler and her elephant ego, and I stop.

I'm making this into something that it's not. I'm sure he thinks that kiss was as weird as I did! Bradley loves the fact that I quite admire escalators. Not me. If he liked me he would have totally made a move now after I kissed him, and he hasn't.

Erin. I wonder if she's seen my vlog. I check Instagram. Sure enough, she's at the top of my feed.

Her latest photo is a STUNNING one of her and her friends. They are angled and contoured immaculately. Erin's cheekbones look like they've been created from a really lovely bit of a marble kitchen counter—pale and perfect with a flash of pink. It must have taken about five attempts to get it just right, but it was worth it. Underneath she's written:

I am BACK!! I decided that you can't let the haters
win and today I had such a wonderful day. After
school some BFFs and I went shopping (YES!
I have more than one BFF!) and all the love was there. I
will share what we bought later (I think you will LOVE
it—but don't get too excited. Just one jacket but a
WONDERFUL one). I just want to thank you ALL so,
so much for your support during this tough time.

I came back from my break to find so many beautiful
messages from all over the world encouraging me to
carry on sharing. And I am going to. You have made
me feel like a total superstar. Thank you SO MUCH.
I will never again let the jealousy of some people stop
what I'm doing or who I talk to. I LOVE YOU x

YET AGAIN there is nothing in that I can moan about. But
underneath it all I know there is a message to me that says, "BACK
OFF, MILLIE. I have the power. I have the masses on my side. If
you attack, I will find not just one but a hundred ways to hurt you."

Right now, I am the stranded whale of the social media world.
Everyone will come to look at me on the beach as I struggle desper-
ately to get oxygen. Some will feel very sorry for me, but they won't
be able to get me back to the sea. And all the time, Erin will be by a
sand dune taking selfies with me in the back, flapping. . . .

And I am getting myself into a right state about everything.

I pick up the phone and call Lauren. FINALLY, she answers!
I tell her what has happened, but she doesn't seem to listen. There
are lots of "yeah"s and "mmmm"s, which are totally unhelpful. She
almost seems in a bit of a diva mood—which is very unlike Lauren.

"The thing is," I say to her, "I need to do SOMETHING!"

"No, you don't," Lauren snaps. Now I'm really worried. She
doesn't get how serious all this is.

"Lauren! All my followers will be waiting for me to respond to
her!"

"No, they won't, Millie. You can do a one-minute-long vlog.
'What to do when you're caught out. Well, you just have to take it

on the chin and move on with it. Thanks. Bye.' That's what you should do."

Lauren sounds angry. Almost . . . nasty.

"You think it's as simple as that?"

"Probably, Millie. Anyway, stuff is going on here, so I've got to go. Bye."

I say, "Okay. Bye!"

But I don't really believe that at all—inside I am broken and absolutely gutted. And what stuff is going on that Lauren can't speak to me about?! That's total spoon behavior from her.

Or . . .

Or perhaps she's been kidnapped, and she's being held hostage and can't talk to me.

Perhaps "stuff" was a code word for really bad stuff involving extremists who want to make the country YouTube-free or Lauren-free or something.

Or perhaps she's cross with me. Though, I can't think why she would be. I've told her everything that's happened with the vlog while she's been away.

Either way, I can't sit here and let my friend become a statistic or fall out with me. I need to go over to her house and find out what's going on. I wonder about taking backup, but in a house full of ghosts and old people, it's better, as Granddad says, to be a lone soldier of fortune. With a phone. I take my phone, obviously. You can't be without that. That would be insane.

#BFFGoneBad

This is scary, and midweek should not be about face-to-face combat. It's a drastic measure, but some things need sorting right now. As I get around the corner to Lauren's house, I start to case the joint. I watched this on a private investigator's vlog once. You assess the hostility and the threat.

I see that Lauren's dad is mowing the lawn, so I decide that perhaps I may have overreacted to any threat, but I was right to check. You can't be too careful.

Lauren's dad can't hear me over the hum of the mower. It's odd, because the grass doesn't need cutting, but you can't argue with gardeners. I know that from Granddad.

I run upstairs to see Lauren. She's sitting on her bed and barely looks at me when I walk in. "Oh, you've remembered that I exist," she says.

"Lauren! What is up with you? Why haven't you replied to any of my messages or been at school? Are you ill? You've been acting like a TOTAL cow."

She gives me a look that she's never given me before, like she's about to explode. Then she sneers, "I'm surprised you've noticed.

You're so in love with those people on your vlog. Or Danny. Or Bradley."

OH. So she isn't in any danger from a terrorist group. She's actually just JEALOUS. This makes me LIVID.

"Well, Lauren. Sorry to tell you this, but people on there actually need me for a bit of good sense and stuff. A bit of—"

Lauren gets off her bed and starts screaming. Actual, total RAGE. "I need you, and I'm actually real! I helped you make that vlog WHAT IT IS! Have you noticed that I'm having the worst time at home ever?! My parents are at war. I don't even know where my mum is right now. My dad isn't speaking to anyone and is mowing dirt. HE IS TRYING TO MOW ACTUAL MUD. I am going through HELL. And all you care about these days is your views. Your views?! Who do you think you are?! WHY DO YOU EVEN BOTHER?! You've been totally taken in by it all, Millie. Everything you say and do is about your YouTube channel and your friends on there. And I was happy to help, but now it's taken over. You don't need my advice. Go and speak to one of your many friends." (Lauren keeps making little quotation marks with her fingers every time she says the word *friends*.) "YOU don't need a best friend. You need a public-relations manager!"

This makes me cross. I've totally been there for Lauren. All the time. Okay, I might have got a bit distracted lately. But she obviously can't deal with the fact that I have different friends and different interests, and YES! I have done something that a lot of—well, some—people are getting comfort from. Perhaps I haven't asked her about stuff as much as I should have, but I'm so cross at her for ruining it all that I end up yelling, "Your parents have been rubbish for years. What's new?!"

Even as I'm saying these words, I know they sound totally awful. Enormous levels of awful, too. But I can't stop saying them. And when I do say them, Lauren goes a funny color.

"You know what, Millie. You're right. Yes, they have been. And you've been really great about it. You've really helped me. But recently, it's just been all about you. Or you and Erin. Who cares what she thinks ALL the time? And also, the way you've been treating Bradley is just . . ."

"Just WHAT?" And this I really want to know, because . . . this will totally prove that Lauren is just being completely HORRIBLE and is really just upset at her mum and dad. That's fine, but be angry at them! Don't have a go at me!

"You KNOW Bradley likes you," Lauren shouts. "You KNOW he does! But you keep on pretending that he doesn't and hanging out with him so he'll help you with your vlog. And if Mr. Sexy Maple Leaf wasn't already dating Erin Breeler, you wouldn't even talk to Bradley, Millie! That's not fair!"

I'm not having this.

"Lauren. We. Are. Friends. Are you saying women can't be just friends with a man? I'm sorry, Lauren, but that is totally unfeminist. Bradley is *responsible for his emotions*, not me!"

(I saw that phrase in an article online—it sounds good.) I'm also trying really hard not to think about the fact that I've snogged him and not told my best friend.

"It's got nothing to do with feminism, Millie! It's got everything to do with not being a cow. You always bring up the clever stuff when you want to win a row or look cool. How about just not being an idiot that only cares about herself and her PROFILE? I know I'm not the only person with parents who have split up, Millie. I know that. But today I'm the only ex–best friend of yours that has. I'm the only person I know who woke up to her mum crying and packing a suitcase and saying 'sorry' repeatedly. My mum left home today! She left my DAD and left HOME! But don't worry—I understand that, to you, YouTube is more important."

Now I feel DREADFUL.

"It's not!" I whisper. "I'm not a mind reader! Why didn't you tell me?"

"I couldn't get a word in!" Lauren says through tears. "And you haven't asked me what's going on in my life for ages. I'm sorry that Erin is not very nice to you, but so what? So you're the person she got today. There will be another one tomorrow. And the next day. That's what Erin does. You can't change it."

I start to think. "Do you really think I've treated Bradley badly?"

Lauren throws her hands in the air. "Oh, we're back to YOU again! Do me a favor, Millie. Just GO! GO! You're not a person I like right now. You've been completely messed up by a tiny bit of fame. HASHTAG DREADFUL USELESS COMPLETELY POINTLESS BEST FRIEND."

I start to cry. Lauren starts to cry.

As I leave, I notice that Lauren's dad has been mowing the same bit of mud during the entire time I've been with her. He didn't see me arrive, and he doesn't see me leave. I think Lauren could get kidnapped and he wouldn't notice. Perhaps I wouldn't notice, either. I'd be too busy uploading or recording or something.

I'm useless.

#TerribleBestFriend. I never thought that would be aimed at me. But it might be true. It IS true. Very true.

#Escalation

Yes. All this has escalated quickly. Not in a Bradley way.

In a bad-without-any-amazing-moving-stairs way.

Back in my bedroom, life seems completely grim. I'm a bad daughter to my mum and a useless friend, I hurt lovely men, I'm a bad feminist or a good one that's bad (I can't decide which), and I've forgotten to give my cat her one-drop flea treatment, and she's currently scratching in a way that says she needs it.

How do I even have the nerve to do an advice vlog?! My life is a total and utter mess. I want to ring my mum, but that will just remind me that I don't get along with her, either. Her answer to everything is to tell me to come home. I can't go back there. I can't go back to that level of clean.

Perhaps I'm a grot, too.

The fact is, I have failed at just about everything. I have upset everyone who has ever been lovely to me . . . and now I am looking at Aunty Teresa, who's standing at the end of my bed dressed as Queen Victoria. She has frills, bum and tum pillow padding, and everything.

"Hello, Mills. Your dad and I have had this idea that we want to put to you . . . we want you to come and join us. Be part of what will become the biggest ghost tour in the country. We want you to do ALL our social media. We thought we could get you to pretend on your advice vlog that you had someone write to you about having a ghost. THEN you get me on to talk about what you do when you have a ghost in your house and THEN, at the end, you say, 'Thank you, Teresa, poltergeist specialist, who organizes the ghost tour every Thursday and Tuesday from six o'clock, concessions available, and if you do book as a group, a can of Coke is included in your entrance fee.' It's not proper Coca-Cola—it's the cheap supermarket stuff—but we don't have to mention that, do we? I don't think so."

Aunty Teresa doesn't realize that I've been crying, so I just say, "I don't think I'll be doing a vlog for a bit."

"Okay," she says, "but there's something else. We'd like you to join us on the ghost tour. You see, we need a younger female character to play a little match girl that dies horribly in Victorian times from being just really cold without a decent duffel coat."

"It's called hypothermia," I say.

"Yeah. That!" Teresa says. "So you just have to basically stand there and moan a bit and say stuff like, 'I'm freezing' and 'Would you like to buy some matches? It doesn't matter if you don't smoke. You can use them to light your scented candles.' What do you think?"

"I don't think they had scented candles in Victorian times." This sounds ridiculous, even for Teresa.

"Whatever!" she says excitedly. "You can freestyle. Shiver a bit. You can moan, too. It'll be really"—Teresa pulls this superserious face and twiddles her fingers—"eerie. . . ."

Usually I would be shouting "NO WAY," but my mouth hurdles

over my brain and says "yes." Perhaps it's about time I did something for someone else. I want to take my mind off everything. Ghosts will do. And let's be honest: I've reached peak dork on the vlog. What could possibly be worse than that?

"Just promise there'll be no photos shared on the Internet. ANYWHERE."

"I can't promise that completely, as anyone can be snapped these days, but I will say no photos of the match girl, as it's dangerous to take photos of our workers whilst they are channeling spirits."

"Just to be clear, Teresa," I say, "I'm not pretending to channel anything. I'm only doing this as a favor."

"I know." Teresa hugs me very tightly. "And I really appreciate it. I know you'll just be doing this for us."

That's not completely the truth, though. Doing something, ANYTHING, will make me take my mind off things. Even if that anything is pretending to be a starving, underage worker in a vintage dress.

"Oh," Teresa adds quickly, "and, by the way, we start tomorrow night. Hope that's okay for you. Here's your tray. All you have to do is tie the ribbons around your neck and pretend to be ill. Try some flour on your face. That got me out of school every week, I looked so ill. I'll leave your costume out for you tomorrow. See you at six o'clock outside the old church that's been converted into a posh block of flats opposite the driving test center."

Teresa disappears very quickly.

I may die a social death but not an actual death. Being a starving Victorian match girl will hopefully remind me that life isn't so bad, though it's terrible at the moment.

I'm having a sensible burst again. I'm still in there somewhere!

#Ghostbusters

For most of Thursday, I opt for a social coma at school.
I'm physically present but not mentally there. Lauren is still away,
and I have enough hiding spots to avoid all boys. I spend all of
lunch in the Zen Loo. Lovely Gracie heard me in the cubicle. I just
told her I was having a nap.

I was glad to get home until I saw what I had to wear for the ghost
tour.

There are no two ways about it. I am dressed up in an old lace
nightie with a cardigan and batter mix on my face. I look like the
ghost of a pancake, not of a little match girl. Also I'm very, very cold.
So I may be dying an actual death, too. Teresa has made sure I'm
on a main road. This is great for personal safety, but not great for
how many people are staring at me. I wish she would hurry up.

Just as I'm seriously thinking of packing everything in and going
home, I hear Teresa and the group of ghost hunters she's with coming toward us. She's telling them that the church couldn't be turned
into flats until they'd rid the place of the ghost of a sad weeping match
girl who had died of cold in the graveyard. I stiffen up, knowing that
this is my cue to start moaning and acting generally very ill indeed.

Teresa turns the corner and says, "Behold the match girl. See her terrible rags and then we will tell the horrible story about how no one would buy her matches and how she died because of the cruelty of Victorian society. And how she haunts these posh flats because she wants to remind the rich people of today that having really nice IKEA lampshades and probably under-floor heating, too, isn't enough. You need to be a NICE PERSON, too."

I know for a fact that Teresa is saying this because she was jealous that she couldn't afford one of the posh flats.

At this point, I say in a really feeble voice, "Buy a match from a poor match girl. Buy a match. . . ."

As I slump like a really ill person, I notice a figure toward the back of the ghost hunter crowd. Staring at me and flashing me a smile that could and would probably bring a very dead person back to life is Danny. And two people who look very like they could be his parents.

And Erin.

And I'm dressed as a match girl with food smeared all over my face.

I've probably had worse days in my life, but I can't remember one.

I wave at Danny. He bounds over to me, leaving Erin with his parents.

"Hello," I whisper, and pull a *this is actually really embarrassing* face.

Teresa growls at me, "Ghosts don't wave at their earthly friends!"

But just as Teresa tries to shoo Danny away, a man in a suit races out from the posh flats and starts yelling, "Oi! YOU! Get lost. You spreading rumors about this place could take ten grand off my property price! Move yourself."

Aunty Teresa shouts, "This is a public right of way, and I can tell people what I like!"

Someone in the crowd yells, "Is this not true, then?"

"Of course it's not true!" the man in the suit says. "She's making money off of gormless tourists like you!"

Teresa goes quiet and then says, "You can't prove that!"

At this point, all the people in the crowd start tutting and go their separate ways. Teresa says, "No . . . No! Look! Look at the match girl! She'll die without your fee."

Just about everyone rolls their eyes at Teresa.

"Why didn't you take the money at the start?!" I ask her.

Teresa is furious. "I didn't think my match girl would start chatting up the customers!"

I am adding Teresa to the doesn't-like-Millie-much-at-the-moment list.

Danny ignores the fact that I have gone bright red under my pancake mix. "Can I buy some matches, please?" Then he winks.

"What are you doing here?" I ask him.

"I like to find out about social history. I like to know the facts about different places."

"Me, too," I say. "For example, I totally know what to do when a randy elk charges you after you've stared at his girlfriend."

"What's that?" Danny says.

"Run!"

I think at this point I am both wise and slightly hilarious.

However, I can see that Danny is wondering why I've started going on about elk.

Why have I started going on about elk?

"Anyway," he says, "we're going for a pizza with my parents. Want to come, too?"

Danny says this very uncomfortably. It's the right thing to do, but it's obvious that he doesn't want me to come. Erin and I—it's just not going to work.

"Er . . . No. I better get home and check that my aunty is okay." I also think eating a margherita dressed as a Victorian match girl may not be a good look.

"Okay," Danny says sort of gratefully. "Catch you another time."

"Yes!" I say, and I wave good-bye to him and Erin. Erin does not wave back. She's too busy taking photos.

Good-bye, perfect man. Matches, elk, and the fact I'm a useless person have come between us, but that is this day. The worst day in history. This is like the last day in Pompeii, when Vesuvius exploded. I am currently breathing in hot volcanic ash of embarrassment and dying. I will be discovered two thousand years from now. They will find my fossilized remains and know that I died of terminal spoon.

I just need to get home and talk to someone . . . anyone.

#OverAndOut

By the time I get home, I'm just over everything and I don't care. I wipe the batter off my face, get changed out of my costume, and go to the shed. Dave follows me in. She's still scratching and disappears behind me to tackle her fleas in peace.

I've learned a lot these last few days. I feel like I could share something REALLY useful. And who cares about followers or trolls or any of it? This could save someone from what I have suffered. It's time for a really REAL vlog. I turn on the camera.

"*'Hashtag Help Me.'*

"*Help me because I NEED help.*

"*I've decided I want to vlog about friendship and relationships and everything and then I'm taking a break from vlogging. And this time I'm going to be totally honest with you.*

"*The fact is, I feel like a liar. I'm giving all this advice and I can't get my own life sorted.*

"*I'm all glowy online, but offline I'm a massive scribble of MESS and MISTAKES. Here's what happened today. Basically I was meant to be acting like a Victorian match girl for my aunty Teresa's ghost tour. And while I'm dressed like that I see . . . someone I really like, and instead of saying something GOOD, I start talking about Canadian ELK. WHY? WHY? WHY? It's like my brain left my body.*

"But on here, I pretend that I know stuff and that I'm the one who can give YOU advice. I can't! I mess almost everything up. And not just boys but . . .

"The IMPORTANT STUFF.

"I know some of you know me or sort of know me. But do you? And do I really know me? The thing is—and please don't think I'm not grateful for all your feedback—but I am spending so much time thinking about this and what I'm going to do on this vlog that I think I'm missing things in front of me. I'm sorry. This sounds so pathetic. And yes, this is a bit of a meltdown, but there's someone in my life who I have let down so badly. Not by failing to be scary on a ghost tour or by talking about Canadian mammals to a boy I like; I have been ignoring someone who really, REALLY needs me. AND someone who really likes me. And I've been . . . well, I haven't been fair.

"I have someone in my life whose parents aren't bad but are useless. Anyway, she has always been there for me, but when I needed to put her first, I didn't. I put this and you first and someone who doesn't deserve to be put first FIRST. And she's been there for EVERYTHING. From the time I got really worried about earthquakes to when I always think I've done badly on every test and exam we've ever done at school. I know I'm sensible, but I'm also a very annoying worrier. You can be both at the same time. Sometimes one leads to another. The more you know, the scarier the world is.

"BUT ANYWAY . . .

"Anyway, the point is, I didn't give her enough time because of THIS world. You. And you are magnificent. You are lovely. I can't say that enough. You're not the problem. It's me. It's simple. I need to just make sure I don't

miss out on people and actual life. I know, I KNOW I sound like my mum.
I probably sound like your mum, too, and, seriously, I'm not giving a lecture
here, and neither am I saying I'm giving this up for good. I am not. I LOVE
doing this. I'm just putting life in the right order for now. The order that
I think it should be in.

"And SEE: This is the real me.

"And I want to say sorry to a person I really hope is watching this."

(I get a bit teary at this point.)

"So this is Hashtag Help, over and out. I'll see you again sometime. Just
please know that I haven't got all the answers and I get a lot of stuff wrong.
I'm off to put it right now. Well, in the morning. It's late now, and my cat
needs her flea treatment. Not glamorous but fact. Bye."

I upload it. This is probably leaving myself very open to lots of things. But I want Lauren to see it. And I want everyone to know that I've messed up.

I collect Dave and go back to my bedroom. Teresa and Dad are working out the new route for the ghost tour. They are thinking of avoiding the posh flats altogether and using mainly graveyards instead. I hear Granddad saying, "The good thing about dead people is that they can't disrupt your ghost tour, and even if they do, that will be a really good thing."

Granddad should vlog. He's definitely the most sensible person in this house.

Just as I'm about to put my head on the pillow, I get a notification that Mr. Style Shame has posted a photo. When I go to his profile, I can't believe what I see.

There is a photo of me as a ghost. I look awful. The filter makes it even worse. I don't know why Mr. Style Shame hates Loz and me so much at the moment. I've done NOTHING to him. He must be a dreadful, sexist pig.

I read what Mr. Style Shame has written:

> Talk about #WashedOut. This side of Halloween,
> the ghost look is NOT attractive. #FrightNight

How would Mr. Style Shame have seen me? There was hardly anyone at the ghost talk. Just a bunch of tourists, Danny, Erin, and . . .

ERIN.

FINALLY I realize that Mr. Style Shame is ERIN. All this time, she's been pretending to be so positive and mindful and wonderful. In reality, she is just a troll with a really big following. She pretends to be a boy, but it's her. It MUST be her. She MUST be stopped.

I comment underneath:

> This is me in this photo, @MilliePorter. I KNOW who
> you are, "MISTER" Style Shame. You've made it
> obvious. You need to stop this NOW. Or I am going
> to tell everyone EXACTLY who you are and EXACTLY
> what you are about.

I lie back on my pillow and think this is the bravest thing I have ever done. I don't care anymore. I've had the worst day EVER. Let Erin say and do what she likes.

I MUST sleep.

#SuperStar

My phone goes off at 6:55 a.m. I've put it under my pillow and the vibrating wakes me up. I can do that. It's Friday. You can sleep all day Saturday. It's Lauren, and she's crying. "I'm SO sorry," she wails.

"No, I'm really sorry," I say. And I've never meant anything more. I am.

"I saw the vlog, Millie—last night. I wanted to come by immediately, but Dad wouldn't let me. I'm so sorry."

"No! It's me," I shout. "I'm sorry!"

And Lauren and I say sorry for the next five minutes because we both are, even though my sorry is more important than hers.

Lauren then starts giggling.

"It's weird, isn't it? You did that vlog, and it was really just for me. So sweet, and yet it's gone viral and everyone in the world has seen it. I could tell that you hadn't planned it. It was perfect. An apology, some good advice, and COMEDY GOLD."

I nearly choke on my tongue.

"What?!"

"It's gone viral, Millie! Didn't you watch it before you uploaded it?"

"No!" I shout. "It said everything I wanted to and I didn't care! I just wanted to make a point about you. I actually, GENUINELY wasn't thinking about shares or follows."

"Go and watch it, Millie," Lauren says. "It is really funny. Like properly hilarious."

"It's not meant to be funny." I feel quite offended.

"But it is," Lauren replies. "It's EPIC!"

I hang up and watch the vlog. I see a very upset and clearly emotional me saying things I really mean, but I do sound a bit like a teacher. In the vlog, I'm so involved in what I'm saying that I completely fail to notice Dave, who has slinked up behind me and spotted Granddad's wading bird calendar, which is lying on the bench behind me.

Dave doesn't like birds. And she really doesn't like ringed plovers. Even paper ones.

When she spots the ringed plover, Dave decides to lift herself up on two legs and dance hypnotically from side to side. She's better than the "Thriller" cat, like she's been trained by the world's best choreographers. She then starts diving up and down on top of the plover, licking the plover, head-butting the plover, and twizzling her bum on the plover.

Someone has already relabeled the video: "INSANE Cat Goes Mad Behind Seriously Upset Girl." That version has over 75,362 views already.

There are loads of comments. Mostly about Dave.

Cat is EVERYTHING

Need Dave. NOW.

Sitting in my pajamas. School starts in four hours.
Worth it.

Fake

THAT CAT IS INSANE

Get cat on *Dancing with the Stars*. Want to see her
samba and argentine tango.

Cat needs own channel

Like if you're watching this when you should be
asleep!

(This comment has 612 likes.)

Like if you're watching this and you'd like to lose
20lbs on the guava diet!

(This comment has no likes.)
Finally, I've gone viral.
For potentially all the wrong reasons, but it's actually very

sweet that some people enjoyed the message and not the sight of a cat doing the rumba while attacking something that looks like it's wearing a feathery balaclava. So maybe Dave's gone viral and I've . . .

I've also got . . . more than 5,680 new subscribers!

I scream! Teresa rushes in and wants to know what's happening. I tell her that I've gone viral. Teresa opens up the window and shouts, "MILLIE IS VIRAL. HEAR HER!!"

Granddad yells from downstairs, "Is it contagious?! I can't risk it. I had shingles two years ago."

The postman shouts from the street, "I'm thrilled, but I can't deliver with this cat threatening me. There are laws against this, you know."

Me and Teresa jump up and down on the bed for a few minutes, then reality slaps me.

The problem is I know that my going viral will lead to the following things:

1. TOTAL laughs at my expense. I will never be able to move on from this, and it will become legendary.
2. Danny deciding that I am just about the worst example of girlfriend material that there could ever be.
3. Granddad getting angry that Dave has trashed his calendar.
4. Mum thinking that something terrible is about to happen to me.
5. Erin . . .

Erin. I check Mr. Style Shame.

The entire account has been deleted.

It must have been Erin. I saw right through her, and she went for the safe self-destruct option. I can't quite believe it.

My phone vibrates.

It's Bradley. He doesn't even say hello.

"You know what you need to do, don't you?" he almost yells. Enthusiasm is unheard of from Bradley (except when it comes to lifts).

"Yes. I'm thinking of moving to Paraguay and changing my name."

"I don't think you need to do that. All you need to do is make a vlog called 'Cats Happen,' where you explain that life, like cats called Dave, is completely unpredictable and you've got to roll with it and get on with it and not worry too much. You can still give great advice. Get Dave in on it. I think it would be really funny. Laugh with the people laughing at you, Mills, and BUILD ON IT."

"Oh, because that's so easy to do—especially with Dave, the biggest cat diva ever!" I say. Bradley gets my inner sarcasm like no one else.

"No," he replies. "It's not easy, but it's the right thing. Seriously. The video is really funny, and you know what? You are . . ."

And I can hear Bradley really thinking about what he is going to say. . . .

"You are really cool in it and kind. And if you read all the comments, it's not just about Dave. It's about how you sound like a genuinely lovely person."

When I start groaning loudly, Bradley shuts me up. "No—you do! You do! Seriously. Millie, this is a real opportunity now. Everyone will be wondering what you're going to do next. So do something brilliant. Make people realize . . . how special you are."

At that moment, I can sense that Bradley feels like he may have gone a bit too far.

"Anyway," Bradley says, "just do it and see what happens. See you soon. Bye . . . superstar."

And Bradley is right. I need to swallow the feeling inside of me that makes me just want to escape by paddling to Paraguay on an inflatable novelty doughnut (Teresa has one), and do a vlog to end all vlogs. But what do I do about Bradley? I don't want to hurt his feelings, but I think I really fancy—

Danny. No, he's not Danny, but Danny is calling. . . .

"Lady viral sensation! How is life?"

(What is it with men not saying "Hello" today?)

"It's interesting," I say calmly. "I've been totally upstaged by a cat."

"The world loves it. I love it. I think you and Dave are both quirky in that really good British way that's actually sort of Canadian, really."

I'm feeling the patriotic sass. "Didn't we have it first, as actually we did technically invent you?"

Danny pauses. "Okay, well, it's probably the Chinese bit of you. OR the French part of you, which is the really cool bit—*La Millie-Millait*." (He says it like a really sexy French boy.)

I have no idea what he means, so I just say, "Bon," which, apart from *le stylo* and *la chaise*, is the only French word I can remember.

"Why I'm calling," Danny sort of stutters, "is . . . Would you like to meet me and talk about whatever YOU want to talk about?"

Things have officially got BIG. SERIOUS. MASSIVE. SCARY.

"What about Erin?"

"We've been hanging out a bit," Danny says, and he sounds like he's telling the truth. "When I first met her, I thought she was really friendly and cute, but she's got hidden depths. If I'm honest, it's the same way a rattlesnake has got hidden depths."

That's what I love about Danny. He's Canadian and naturally knows lots about horrible, dangerous, exotic animals.

Danny carries on.

"But I wanted to tell you, Erin told me yesterday that she runs Mr. Style Shame. I saw your comment. You guessed correctly. After that post last night, I pretty much knew it could only be her. It was dumb of her, really. Honestly I don't really want to be associated with someone who runs an account like that. I just think it's nasty. She's got a really nasty streak. I don't like that. And her Instagram was a bit much as well. Not that I'm Mr. Gorgeous or anything. I'm not, but she was . . . she is . . . jealous of you, because she knows I think you are funny and . . . cute."

I don't say anything. I can't quite believe all this is happening.

"Anyway," Danny says nervously, "would you like to do something on the weekend? Say on Saturday afternoon? We could get ice cream from that little Italian place on the high street? I read a great blog post about it."

I surprise myself by what I say.

"Danny, that sounds lovely. I'd really like to, but I've just got to sort a couple of things out first. Can I message you later about it?"

"Sure," he says. "Speak to you in a bit."

I feel sensible again. I feel like I just need . . . time. Time to work this all out.

I take a big breath. I need to get ready for school, or I'm going to be really late, but I also want to see what Erin has posted on HER account recently. Yes! I know. I should get over it, but I can't.

Erin's most recent post is an Instagram photo of her in kitten ears. AGAIN.

> These are the sort of cats I like. They don't shed hair
> everywhere. They are easily controlled and they
> make you look really cute.

She hasn't got that many likes. People must have realized that SHE was the person making their fashion lives HELL. If they don't, everyone will know at school in about two hours this morning.

I think a nonhuman may have finally beat Erin. Dave the cat. YouTube superstar. Rebel. Icon. Mess maker. SLAYER OF THE BREELER.

I'm not stupid. Erin will be back and probably worse than ever. This is real life, and real life is complicated. Bad girls sometimes win, but . . . I think I've won this part of the war. Well, Dave has, technically, but I am her commander in chief.

#IRL

When the history of our time is written, they might call
this the greatest Friday ever. Everyone's been giving Erin massive
evils. There's even a new phrase at school—the Evil Erin. It means
you MAJOR death-stare someone and make them feel AWFUL.
But I'm trying to be realistic. Everyone knows now that she's
Mr. Style Shame, but she's still gorgeous and everyone will eventually forgive her and she'll be back.

I don't care. Lauren and I are friends again, AND people think
my cat is seriously cool. And I think that because of what people
have said at school today, Dave and I need to do one FINAL vlog.
If only I could find her.

On the way to the shed, Granddad tackles me. "I've noticed,
Millie, that you spend a huge amount of time getting the perfect
self-photograph or the perfect 'vog' whilst time is passing you by.
Have you tried actually sitting with people and talking to them
face-to-face?"

"That's life now!" I tell Granddad gently. "And it's *selfie* and
VLOG."

"Whatever," Granddad snaps. "But I hope you also realize that life is happening now. Real life." And he pokes me in the shoulder. "Put your phone down—it's not the be all and end all of the universe. Another thing—boys are not always playing games. They are confused, too, you know. And don't go full-on. Leave some mystery."

This is some of the lecture I have heard Granddad give to Teresa many times. It's his speech from the last century. The best thing to do is to nod and say, "Yes!"

He may have a point about the phone, though. But I can think about that after I've done my vlog.

"And I'm not happy with my ripped-up calendar, Millie, but I will just have to live with it."

"Sorry, Granddad," I say, and bow my head. He's right. A destroyed plover is a slightly tragic thing to see. "I'll buy you a new one for Christmas."

When I open the shed door, Dave appears from nowhere and darts her way in. It's like she's a celebrity and she knows it.

I sit on the big chair, and Dave dives onto the space next to me. She curls her tail around the front of her body and sits quietly in front of the camera. I'm feeling a mixture of brave, going-to-be-sick, terrified, and excited. I start filming. . . .

"Hello! It's me, Millie, and this is Dave, and yes, I purposefully have her in the shot this time.

"So obviously lots of you saw the video, and lots of you are still seeing the video where I'm trying to make a serious point about looking after your friends, and Dave—her name is Dave, by the way—decided to freak out in the background and try to kill my granddad's calendar.

"I was, as you can imagine, feeling totally embarrassed and was genuinely thinking about moving abroad and changing my name until I realized

that YouTube is global anyway. Besides, I can't do that as I have a family who loves me loads despite being completely insane, and they would miss me. As would my lovely friends, too, including my friend Bradley. Do go and check out his vlog about escalators. I KNOW it doesn't sound cool, but you may actually really come to appreciate them. I sort of have. Plus it was my brilliant friend Bradley who said I should just get back on here and say look—you can't tell cats what to do. And this is my advice about cats and life in general. You can't control any of it, and that is really, really scary. So what you have to do is just let mad cats and mad life do their thing and go with it. You've just got no control. . . .

"Remember the very first vlog I did? It's just the same thing.

"For example" (and I point to Dave and command) *"Dave, attack the bird!"*

(Dave does nothing.)

"Dave, go on two legs and pretend you're on a TV dance competition!"

(Dave does nothing.)

"You see? No control. So this is me, Millie Porter—stress-head, Queen of Sensible, control freak, in charge of a completely unpredictable, uncontrollable life and cat—saying that you should try to chill out as much as you can. Even if you own a mad feline. Bye! Hashtag Help is out of here FOREVER!"

Dave still does nothing.

I upload and feel sort of good about things.

As I message Danny to say I will meet him on Saturday, Dave starts to act odd. Typical. When I need her to act calm, she acts strange.

Mum is staring in through the shed's tiny window. She sees me looking, storms in, and grabs hold of my hand.

"Mills. I've got something to tell you, and it's very important."

#Revelation

The terrible part of me wants it to be that she has split up with the Neat Freak. The thing about love is that it makes you just a little bit mad, and Mum should know. Love has condemned her to a life of bleach, but there are worse things I suppose. I keep all those bad feelings to myself.

"No—I haven't split up with Gary."

Why can she always mind-read me with such total rightness?!

"No. It's about my head. You see, Millie, your head is like mine, and I know what's going on with it."

Parents are very worrying when they say things like this, because they almost certainly have no idea how you are feeling and how your brain is working.

Mum can sense my doubts. "No, really, I can. We've got the same brain. And the brilliant thing about our brains is that they're clever and they make good decisions. That seems boring now, but I promise it won't be boring when you're thirty-eight."

Even I don't care about being thirty-eight, but I go with it.

"But I want to tell you about the trees and me."

I am seriously worried.

"The thing is," Mum continues, "when I was little, there was this thing that was killing loads of trees. It was called Dutch elm disease. And I totally got it into my head that Dutch elm disease could spread to humans."

I don't want to sound insensitive. "Mum, where is this going?"

"Listen!" she says, sounding very irritated. "I got myself into a total state. And all these trees were dying, and there was no Internet. You couldn't just google things. You had to go to the library and grown-ups told you NOTHING. So I thought I was dying. With the trees."

I'm confused.

"So you're saying you were green and environmentally friendly before most other people."

"No, Millie. I'm saying that I was worried about things and GOT ANXIETY like you get. I HAD IT. We didn't call it anxiety then. It was called . . . just being pathetic. BUT IT WASN'T. And your brain, I CAN SEE, has the same thing. A lot of people have it. Usually very clever people who are connected and level-headed and . . ."

"Preach, Mum, preach," I say—a bit sarcastically, I have to admit.

"No, I need you to really listen, Millie."

And I can see that Mum is tearing up a bit, so I shut up. That is sensible.

"When you've got a brain like that, you have to learn to look after it and train it. And you don't have to pretend to be strong when you aren't feeling strong. It's fine to say, 'I don't know what to do.' It's fine to say, 'I can't cope.' It's fine to say, 'I've started this brilliant vlog,' and, Millie, it is great, by the way, but actually it's fine to say,

'I don't know the answer to every question and right now I just need to keep MY head together.'"

"Is that what you did?" This is a major revelation.

"No." Mum looks down. "And I paid for it. I ended up being very poorly. In my head. I was in the hospital. With this . . ."

Mum taps her head.

It's so odd! I have never ever thought my mum could be the sort of person that would ever be mentally ill. In a silly way, I thought she was a bit barking for going out with Gary the Neat Freak, but that's it. Not THIS.

"Mum, I'm so sorry. Why didn't you tell me?"

"You're clever and sensible, Millie, but you don't give children more than they can actually cope with. It's not fair. When your dad and I split up, we were very sure that both of us were going to make it as easy for you as possible. So you never saw the time when I threw an entire packet of premium pork-cider-and-apple sausages at him."

Mum laughs. "It's funny now." She giggles. "It wasn't funny then."

Why do adults always throw groceries at each other? Wet sponges would be a wiser, better option.

"You're a beautiful, clever, brilliant girl. It's lovely that you want to help people and just give people some of YOU, because YOU are wonderful. I'm not saying stop doing it—what I am saying is that you don't have to fix people. It's YOUR job to take care of your head and not bring anyone else down. That's all. Anything else is a bonus."

After all this, there is one question that is mainly in the front of my head.

"*Can* you get Dutch elm disease?"

"No." Mum shakes her head. "But you can get splinters from trying to cuddle trees and make them better. And yes, I did. And yes, I recycle. And that's why my car is electric. You find your little ways to make things . . . better. Because I still watch the news and think . . . well . . . There's always been what you would call 'twonks,' Millie—twonks in your life and twonks on the news, and you—"

"I get it, Mum." I look at her. This has been a major lecture session, but . . . it has helped a bit.

"Mum, if you ever want to talk about what happened—"

Mum interrupts and goes all hard-faced. "Millie, I don't. It happened. I got through it. And look at me now. A lovely daughter"—she gets hold of me and hugs me—"and a great job and a man that DOES THE HOOVERING."

I shake my head. Mum knows what I am thinking. "Believe you me, Millie, I know Gary seems like a pain, but a man that enjoys the feel of a dustpan and brush, and sends you flowers all the time, makes you laugh, and is kind, is a pretty good man. But that's a chat for another time. Men are wonderful, but they are not the solution. Or women. You may be a lesbian. Which is fine, by the way."

By this stage, it's beginning to feel like I'm listening to a really uncomfortable speech that Mum has planned for years and years, but anyway.

She gives me a hug. I'm proud. And then she pinches my arm. "All I am saying is, just don't forget the people who are around you. I'm not saying the people on there"—her finger slams on the glass screen of my phone a little too hard for my liking—"I'm not saying the people on there aren't lovely, but can they do this?"

And Mum gets me in this incredible boa-constrictor-squeeze-hold cuddle, which is both lovely and slightly scary at the same time.

While she is holding me tight, I squeak, "Mum. Can I come home? I'll try to keep things tidy for Gary."

Mum pulls me closer and says, "Whenever you want, Millie. In my eyes, you NEVER left. And I think it will be better this time. You can have the Wi-Fi on till ten o'clock. And I've already had a proper chat with Gary about McWhirter. It's your home, too, and he has to get used to your crumbs. And from now on, I'll try to make Thursday night Mum-and-Millie night."

We have a little cry until Mum wiggles her head from side to side, does a big sniff, and says, "Now, Millie Porter—hashtag helper or whatever you call yourself! I need to go and have dinner with my boyfriend, who is taking me to the cinema tonight in GOLD class! I'll get wine and food, too. My days of popcorn and half a vat of Diet Coke are gone. Tell you what, Millie—if you want to work out what a good man is, then find a man who really thinks about YOU rather than what they would like to do. Good-bye. I love you. And remember that I'm here"—and she thumps my hand against her heart—"ANYTIME you want me."

I give my mum another HUGE cuddle and thank her, but I don't ask what I really want to ask.

I want to ask Mum about men, but I don't. In a way, I don't want to because just thinking about men is largely very confusing indeed.

I know Bradley likes me. In fact, I think I now have two boys who like me. But how do you tell one of them that you actually want to be with someone else? I don't want to leave the heart of either one lightly smashed. Won't I end up feeling dreadful? Won't he feel rejected?

But I have to do something. Lauren was right. I have been a bit awful about it all.

I've been not exactly great about a lot of things. And now I've got to tell everyone in this house that I want to move back in with Mum.

I'm sure Dave knows already. She's glued herself to my ankle. She's made herself into a furry shoe.

#GrandSad

It takes a while to get everyone together in the front
room. As usual, there is a big mess of people doing random and
largely pointless things in different parts of the house. When I yell
that I need to speak to everyone together, though, they all eventually come. Teresa thunders down the stairs, Dad tries to barge Teresa
out of the way, and Granddad shuffles in holding a bubble level. He
often holds a bubble level. It's like his ultra-accurate, comforting
teddy bear.

I look at them. They are all lovely in a strange way. I'm very lucky.

"Thank you so much for letting Dave and me stay here, but I've
decided that it would probably be best if I moved back in with Mum.
Not today, but, say, next week sometime. She really misses me, and
I really love being . . ."

I can sense huge tears not just pricking but stabbing the sides of
my eyes. My throat goes tight. I can see all of them smiling at me,
trying to help me along, but it just makes me feel more guilty and
sad. I hear myself squeaking. I sound like a really sick door.

Dad sees that I'm in trouble, gets up, and hugs me. "Mills," he
says, "I totally get it. You don't have to explain yourself. I've told

you before and I will tell you again—you've got a room here whenever you need one. Even if it's just for a night."

Teresa stands behind Dad, nodding solemnly. "Yes!" she whispers. "And don't worry about Dave. My friend Julie just gave birth, and she is using craniosacral therapy to help her baby relax. All you do is massage the top of the head. I bet it works with cats, too. I am more than happy to come by your mum's house and work with Dave's feline acupuncture stress points to help her settle back in."

Even though I know Teresa is deadly serious, this makes me laugh.

Dad giggles, too, but I see a flash of gray wool as Granddad, with his bubble level and his cardigan full of holes, slinks out of the room. He doesn't say a word. He just disappears.

I look at Teresa and Dad. "Don't worry," I say. "I'll go and talk to him."

Dad gives me an arm squeeze and mumbles, "You know, you're his favorite person on this earth. He'd perhaps never say it, but you are."

I think I know this, too. I just want to give Granddad a huge hug. I know where he'll be.

Even though he takes things slowly, Granddad can move fast. When I get to the shed, he's holding a hammer, gazing at it like it's a really cute puppy.

"Funny thing, hammers," he finally says.

I don't know what to say to this. I don't think there is a right answer to how strange hammers are.

I go to speak, but, before I can, Granddad says quietly, "I'll be glad to have my shed back, but I'll miss you, you know."

This makes me totally tear up again. I'm not moving to the moon, but I love my granddad. I put my arm around his shoulder, and he grabs my hand. It's all lovely and uncomfortable at the same time, so I blurt out something to make us smile.

"Actually, I'd still like to use the shed if that's okay."

Granddad jokily shakes me off and shouts, "Oh! You would, would you, Miss Superstar? Well, I might start charging for this vog studio."

I don't bother correcting him. He's being really sweet and funny and I love him.

"Just one thing, Millie," he adds. I can tell he's turned serious.

"When you're giving people bad news, like you did today, always shoot straight with your arrow. Don't be brutal with the truth, but . . ."—he hesitates—"shoot straight and true."

I think he means *be nice but tell it like it is*. I tell him I will.

I know I've got to put a lot of things straight. Things like Bradley.

#LikeANiceArrow

I wait till Saturday morning and then I message Bradley.

> **Do you want to meet up?**

Bradley replies like he has been sitting on his iPhone.

> **If you can fit me in, global celebrity. See you at 2 at the mall**

I look at my vlog. Loads of views already, and it's only been up for half an hour. People must be looking as soon as they get notifications. This is great, but . . .

Aunty Teresa comes in and tells me that, with my dad's help, she has finally got her ice-cream van finished and is thinking of rebranding it as "Ice Scream" and using it as part of her new nowhere-near-the-posh-flats ghost tour.

This is actually a great idea, but I still can't think of anything but Bradley. I'm really nervous.

When I get to the shopping center, the clock moves as slowly as

Dave the cat when you want her to do something, and then finally, eventually . . .

It's 2:00 p.m. and forty-three seconds.

I see Bradley. He's never late.

In almost silence, Bradley and I go and sit down on his favorite bench between his favorite lift and the double-fronted Otis lift that secretly goes to the basement if you press the right buttons.

I stutter, "Bradley . . . I, er, really like you. . . ."

"I know," he says, "but you really, REALLY like Danny. Mr. Normal. And I suppose he doesn't bore you with lifts. And escalators."

"Actually, Bradley." I stare at him intently. "I want you to know that I do have a newfound respect for lifts that I never had before I met you. I like to think that if I can open one mind up to the gift of lift engineering, then . . ."

Bradley looks gutted.

"Don't tell me. You should never have kissed me."

"No. I shouldn't have," I whisper. The fact that I did makes me a cow.

"Don't worry." Bradley sighs sarcastically. "What girl can resist such geek talk? And now I suppose you just want to be friends."

This is awful. I cannot describe how terrible I feel. I would HATE it if someone did this to me.

"Please, can we?" I whisper.

"No," Bradley snaps. Then he becomes gentler. "No. No. No. It doesn't work like that. Because right now I want to be horrible to you and say the worst things ever, and seriously, I just need to go before I say something, because . . . just . . . just—I need to go."

Bradley disappears into a Sigma Solon MRL (he's taught me a lot). The doors shut behind him really slowly. You can't slam a lift. That's the problem.

Horrible. Horrible. Horrible.

That's how I feel.

I call Mum and explain. I just need some advice right now.

"Did you mean to hurt him?" Mum asks.

"Of course not!" I shout.

"No! But you still did, Millie, and that's life. He'll be okay after a while. Male pride is a very complicated thing. In fact, ANY pride is a very complicated thing. You're going to hurt people, and people are going to hurt you. But you can't live a lie. Look at Lauren's parents. Hearts rule where heads fear to tread, Millie. Get used to it."

In the middle of a shopping center, I ask Mum a very important question. "Mum, does this get easier?"

"Oh, no!" Mum says, and she's brutal. And then she corrects herself a bit. "Yes, it does, darling. You learn to manage it a bit better. And you can see the problems galloping down the road before they knock you over. Usually. Not always. But here's a tip—don't you DARE share what happened with that boy ANYWHERE. NOTHING. No vlog. No 'vaguebooking' or whatever it's called. Some things, Millie, are not and never will be for public consumption. Sharing YOUR thoughts is one thing. Sharing the pain of others without their permission is just cruel. DO NOT do it. You're not my Millie, the girl I know and love, if you do."

I know she's right. Even though it would make the best subject matter ever for a vlog.

"Don't worry, Millie. Bradley will find someone else! And then YOU'LL be jealous and wonder what is happening and if you've made the right decision. But you should be happy that such a lovely young man—and he sounds like one—has found happiness."

And I will be—it's just that . . .

You know, when I started this whole thing, I thought I knew loads. But it's by sharing what I thought was loads that I realized I've got quite big gaps of things I have no clue about. Although escalators now aren't one of them.

Life is very confusing. Or, as Granddad says wrongly, trying to sound very clever indeed, this whole thing seems to have led to a great deal of "confusement."

Now I've just got to wait around for Danny. Two boys in one day. I feel slightly cow, and I hope Erin isn't around. I hope no one is around. I might go and hide at the florist's. It's like a mini jungle in there.

#Danny

I see Danny floating toward me, and honestly, I know
I've made the right decision. Don't hate me. I know this is shallow,
but he is GORGEOUS.

"Hello, my lady of global fame. How are you?"

"Well, not really *global* fame. But. Yes. Doing quite well vlogging-
wise. I'm good. I wondered—"

"Yes," he says. "The answer is 'yes.' I would love to buy you an
ice cream."

What follows is a stupendous kiss. It is the equivalent of a million likes on every social media network ever. A mass of emoticons
and hearts and a huge THUMBS ALOFT firework that sends me
off my head. Do they teach kissing in schools in Ontario? I think
they must, because Danny has elevated the kiss to a school subject,
passing with the best grade possible.

It's a kiss that makes me feel brave and brilliant and . . .

"Danny, I really like you."

We kiss AGAIN. This is truly magnificent.

"I really like you, too, Miss Porter, problem sorter. Can I take
you to Wagamama this evening?"

I would love to go and slurp noodles with Danny, but I have to be honest. "I'd love to, Danny. I can hang out this afternoon, but there's something really important I've got to do this evening."

Danny looks disappointed.

"Look: I really like you, Danny. I'm thinking you want to sort of try to be my boyfriend . . . thing. . . ."

Danny smiles. "Yeah."

"Well, me, too. I mean, I want to be your girlfriend, but—"

Danny interrupts, "But you'll have lots of options now that you're a global sensation."

This takes me totally by surprise. "Oh no! It's not that. The thing about vlogging is, it's wonderful, but . . . I just want to enjoy people who I can actually . . . poke in the arm."

I jab Danny's bicep. He must work out. It's tough, but he pretends my poke hurt.

"I've just learned that to be a great vlogger, I've also got to . . . I wanted to be famous, and I tried a bit too hard and then when Dave did what she did, it just proved it."

"It proved what?" Danny asks me.

"I'm not sure." This makes us both laugh.

"Can we do something tomorrow?" I ask him. "Maybe the cinema? I'll message you. But there's just something I've got to do now that's really important, and it's important that I do it tonight."

I can see Danny still looks hurt, so I tell the truth. "It's not vlogging or anything. It's family. Do you know what I mean?"

Danny grins and winks. "I know exactly what you mean. I'm away from a lot of mine, and I miss them. You want to make sure you catch up!"

"That's just it!" I say.

Danny and I then have another terrific kiss. When I open my eyes, two beautiful pools of lovely are smiling back at me.

Sorry. Vomfest. But the boy is magical. "Message me," he whispers, and blows a kiss.

It's hard to leave such a hero of pure beauty.

But there's someone I really need to spend time with.

#GirlTime

"Mills, HOW DID IT GO?!" Lauren screams through the phone. "I've been sitting here, actually feeling sick. What happened? What did they say? Was it basically *Hollyoaks*?"

Lauren sounds as if she is about to explode. I'm back home and more chill.

"I wondered if you wanted to come by tonight and eat pizza and try to get Dave to do tricks for pepperoni."

"For your vlog?" she asks.

"No. Just for us," I say. "'*The sisters in crime, talking in rhyme. . . .*'"

Lauren picks up our rap that we made up when we were eight years old. "'*Don't eat lime. Don't taste fine.*'"

We both finish it together: "'*Give up talking. Just do a little mime.*'"

It's RUBBISH, but it's our theme song, and we start giggling a lot.

"Can I come by now?" Lauren asks. "My mum is back, and it's like a war zone again."

I tell her "yes" and that I will see her in ten minutes.

While I'm waiting for Lauren, I look at the comments on my latest vlog and nearly drop dead.

> Hello, Millie. You can see by my verified account that
> I represent some of this country's biggest vloggers.
> I'd be interested in talking to you. And your cat. I
> think you are both wonderful. Thanks. Lydia Portancia

This is BIG. Really BIG. I mean, we are now talking about someone who could really take me on. Move things forward. Someone who . . .

Someone who can wait.

Tonight is about my best friend. We'll discuss it later. Perhaps. For the moment, everything can wait. I need major time with the Loz.

I think the key to a sensible life is just putting all the cutlery in the right space and using it at the right time. Don't you?

That and having a cat that doesn't think she's a trapeze artist. I can see Dave walking along the washing line and every so often swinging around it. And no, I'm not filming it. Not now. But maybe check my vlog later . . .

Acknowledgments

Thank you, as ever, to the usual suspects. With special love to the legendary Jordana "Retainer Linda Hamilton alike" Green, Jo-Anne Green, and Gracie Upton.

Lenah Valley Post Office forever.

Want to know what happens next?

Keep reading for an excerpt! ⟹

#FelineFash

It was the hot dog that did it. Definitely.

Generally, you can't have your cat wearing something made of pork on its head without people asking some serious questions about your life. If *your* pet has ever worn your lunch, you'll know what I mean. It's a game changer.

The thing is, eating is difficult when you're thinking hard. You just trust your body to do its chewy thing. The problem was my jaw had kind of skipped after my brain and checked into Hotel La-La Land. My mouth and eyes really didn't notice that an entire frankfurter had somersaulted from a bun. I just kept chomping on the carbs, staring into space whilst my cat did a runway show into the kitchen with some seriously avant-garde headgear.

I only noticed when Mum said, "Millie. Dave is modeling your dinner. Any thoughts?"

Then she gave one of her "all-seeing oracle" parental looks. You know the sort of thing. The "I know you're worried about something but you're not telling me because you're too worried and now *I'm* worried and basically THIS IS A GLOBAL WORRY PANDEMIC" kind of looks.

My mum can tell a lot from a half-a-second stare. It's her special talent. Face reading, guilt-tripping, and getting things out of you that you don't want to talk about. I think the FBI needs her. She'd crack anyone in minutes.

I tried to get her off my case by asking her if she'd managed to get her phone out and record Dave doing her thing for a vlog but Mum said, "No. Creating great content is of no concern to me. It's even less of a concern to me when I think my little girl might be working herself up into a state about things."

There was another epic "drill into my brain" gaze, but at that point Dave sashayed back into the room with a sausage behind her. Mum was distracted, mainly because Dave looked like she should be on the cover of *Vogue*. You've never seen a cat work it with such total conviction. She was Gigi Hadid, but with a tail and a flea collar.

I took my chance then. "I need to go and get my stuff from Dad's place," I snapped very quickly. That's your only hope in a situation like this. Deflecting.

Mum kept looking at Dave, but said firmly, "Okay, Millie, but when you come back we need an honest chat. Anxiety doesn't just steal sausages. It's a thief of your time and your happiness. And it's something . . ."

At that moment Dave jumped onto my lap and dropped a gherkin into my palm. I didn't know I'd lost that, either.

Yes, Mum. We can have a chat. I just need to get things straight in MY head first. And that may take a while. In fact, it may take forever.

But I didn't say that to her. I just gave her a hug, threw Dave the rest of my hot dog bun, and left. Dave loves buns. We call bread "sliced cat-bohydrate" in our house.

I've just realized I'm still holding the gherkin. Random sliced gherkins in your hand usually mean something is not quite right with the world. Let me try to explain what. I don't think it makes me sound very nice, but it's the truth.

When I'm on my own and walking I can think. My feet are smarter than my jaw; they can do their job really well without me worrying about them. When people ask me what my favorite part of my body is I ALWAYS say my legs. It's not how they look (quite skinny calves, BIG thighs, freaky tall toes I've inherited from Dad), it's what they do.

My brain needs some love, you can tell. It's like when you accidentally leave your glass underneath the Coke dispenser and then you get distracted by a cute dog outside (don't tell Dave). You look around and, all of a sudden, you're creating a mini Niagara Falls. I'm like that. I'm overflowing with everything.

Mum, who has a head like mine, says at times when you feel like your brain is about to burst, write down the facts. Not the things you *think* might happen. JUST the facts. You don't need a laptop, a phone, or a pen. You doodle it all down in your head.

- I'm moving back in with my mum and her neat freak boyfriend, Gary. I moved out a few months ago because he made my life impossible, as he wants to ban dust and grime globally. Also, my mum can be a dictator. A benevolent and low-level one, but she still has some power-hungry tendencies. However, NOW we've agreed to compromise. I will try to keep my room clean (well, clean-ISH), stop making epic biscuit crumb bombs (Gary's description, NOT mine) and stop Dave from surfing on Gary's robot vacuum cleaner (impossible. Dave is a speed freak, a celebrity stunt cat, and fears no one and nothing—not even surprise frankfurters). I'm looking forward to it. I've missed my mum. YES, she's too strict, but she's basically a feminist warrior with epic taste in ankle boots. Don't get me wrong, I've loved living with my dad, Granddad, and Aunty Teresa. It's been great getting to know Dad a bit more. He's been in other countries for a lot of my life, and I do feel like I've missed out. Aunty Teresa has also been living abroad in a way—just in her head on her own planet. I think Granddad has really enjoyed having me around. He may be an epic sexist stuck in the last century, but he appreciates my streak of sensible. I love all of them, but I'd like to be in a house with an actual lock on the front door that works. It's also difficult to watch TV when two people in their forties are having a danceoff to Bruno Mars. I just want more . . . *order.* Yes, I'm tragic. I like things on the quiet side and it's difficult to get peace when Aunty Teresa's fixer-upper ice cream truck is playing "Pop Goes the Weasel" in the front yard. Also, my dresser is an exercise bike that no one uses. So, yes, I'd like something a bit more . . . normal. I will miss them, though. It's good to know some adults stay a bit silly and don't think that having a clean kitchen sink is the peak of their existence. Gary's permanent aftershave is a mixture of Versace for Men and white vinegar.

- I have a boyfriend. Danny. It took a while for us to get together. I was confused or he was. We BOTH were, I guess. It all got a bit weird BUT now we are an official trademarked item. He's funny, kind, and completely owns his own brand of Canadian handsomeness. He also has a pencil case in the shape of a llama and he doesn't care what anyone thinks. Nothing ever seems to faze him. He's permanently chill—like a gorgeous refrigerator but with warm arms. In the past few weeks he's been incredible because honestly, with everything that's been going on, things have been stressful. Danny is phenomenal at just making things seem manageable. He's an accidental life coach. You give him a mountain and he makes it feel like a tiny hill (in the good way). I've really appreciated that AND I am NOT being a pathetic girl. I've just needed good friends who make me laugh—and he does. He's also an epic kisser. Yeah, Danny is almost perfect. Except for liking noodles with too much garlic, but I've learned to live with that. Extra-strong mints are our friend.

This is the hard one. I'll just try to say it quickly.
I can't say it quickly. Who am I kidding? This is BIG.

- I went viral. Well, me and Dave the cat went viral. She went crazy behind me when I was doing a really personal vlog and now we've got real human followers and someone who manages "life content creators" (why do these people always use fancy names?) wants to meet me to discuss how she can help me become "even bigger." Lauren, my BFF, thinks this is wonderful. Erin, previously known as Lady Uber Cool who was sensationally outed as the person behind the most EVIL Instagram account EVER, suddenly wants to be besties with me. My granddad is a tiny bit impressed even though he has no idea what it all means. I was just another rando recording videos in a shed and now, because of a bizarre feline accident, I'm big. And it's what I want. I'm viral and I want to keep being viral. Mum gets it. She says this is AMBITION and an acknowledgment of my innate skill set and I should EMBRACE it. I want to be a success. It is FINE to say that. Viral. It's everything I wanted and it's EVERYTHING I want but now that it's happened . . .

I'll be really honest with you. It's all got a bit intense. The truth is, I'm having trouble coping with this whole "being quite great all the time" thing.

What I've found out is that I can cope with being useless. That sounds insane, I KNOW, but it's sort of fine to me. Even dreadful, crushing defeat and "throw my lunch all over the cafeteria whilst everyone watches and then applauds" mistakes. I just go to my special Zen Loo cubicle for five minutes, take some deep breaths, and start again. But success? Success is HARD. I now understand why celebrities do wild stuff when they get even a tiny bit famous. It's ODD when people you don't know like you. The whole world is applauding you and telling you you're brilliant, but inside you don't feel any different to how you felt a week ago. You just want to say "Dear World. I'm still the same Millie. I haven't got a clue what I'm doing and I don't know what I'm going to do next either and what if it all goes wrong and . . ."

I'm taking deep breaths. HUGE ones. Mum told me she used to be this way. It's anxiety. She learned to manage it. So can I.

I know what you're thinking, because I'd be thinking the same. Millie, shouldn't you be in Vegas with a massive billboard and lots of backup dancers in sequined leotards? Because YOU have become a diva with a capital D in big lights. What a brat. What's up with me?! It's like when people post a selfie of themselves crying. Liam Whitehead did one when his skateboard lost its wheel. It's good to see a guy comfortable with his full-on emotions, but we felt total sympathy for him anyway! We didn't need a photo of his big red face with a filter that made him look like a really angry opossum with conjunctivitis.

Like Liam's crazy eye, this is probably something I shouldn't share with anyone because everyone will just start screaming STOP BEING AN ATTENTION SEEKER!

I KNOW this situation is wonderful. THIS IS ACTUALLY ALL A DREAM. If this were a film, I just would have run off to a massive piece of music, all smiles after a big Danny kiss, epic filter, skin LUMINOUS, probably riding a unicorn.

But this is real life and I'm waiting for disaster. In *my* sort of movie I'm the person shouting on the beach that the tsunami is heading straight for us. Everyone else ignores me and carries on sunbathing and eating fries.

And when the tsunami finally arrives, it's just a tiny wave that knocks over one beach parasol and slightly splashes a lifeguard.

I need to sort myself out. And fast. What I'm doing isn't wrong. Influencers need to be sure of themselves. It's feminist to go after what you want. It's basically being Beyoncé and she can do no wrong. At times like this, I need my Jay-Z.

#WearATree

Danny's mum likes me. I can tell. When she opens the front door she basically drags me in and smiles from ear to ear. "Oh! Here she is! The acceptable face of cat lady!" she shouts. I think Mrs. Trudeau is also relieved, as Danny's last serious girlfriend was mainly mascara-based and there's only so long you can talk about lash length. "Millie!" she whispers. "He's upstairs! Tell him that he needs to pack SOMETHING. He can't JUST wear branches. However much he'd like to."

This makes no sense, but the Trudeau household often doesn't. It's a bit out there.

When I get to Danny's room he's looking at an empty bag.

"Hello, Mills! What do you pack for a holistic spa weekend? I'm thinking hardly anything. I might just wear foliage!"

I stare at him. "Yeah, your mum is worried about that. I don't think branches will work for you. When are you going?"

Danny looks at me with a slightly folded-up face. "Er. Tomorrow. Did I not mention it?"

"No, you didn't," I say casually. My mouth is casual. In my brain, I am not casual in any way. I am annoyed. This is Danny. I love that he's so relaxed, but sometimes this means he lives in an extreme chill bubble. He forgets to tell me key details about his life. It's not that he doesn't care, he just floats around the earth a lot. It's Aunty Teresa disease—just a less severe case.

Danny puts his arm around me. "You're annoyed," he says. "I can tell."

Danny isn't intimidated by strong women, so I serve it up in a brilliant but not hysterical way.

"It *would* be nice to know where you are going to be. I do actually like spending some time with you. I'm not being overdramatic. I just love having a laugh with you. And you get the vlog thing even though you don't really get the vlog thing."

Danny isn't really into social media. He can check his phone twice a day and not be completely itchy about it.

"Sorry, Mills." Danny sighs. "Fair enough. Now, do you think I can just get away with a handful of leaves and some mud?"

He says this with a wink. He makes me laugh a lot. However, at times like this, I can feel my no-nonsense mum invading my brain and it's fantastic.

"I'm not organizing your wardrobe for you. Pay me to be your stylist and I'll help. Until then you're on your own."

"Anyway," I say, "I've got to go and see my family."

Danny hugs me very hard and we have a superb kiss. We have perfected this. We're A-list kissers. "Have a great weekend!" he whispers. "Be you. Be brilliant and go for it. Do a fantastic vlog about bad boyfriends who don't tell their partners where they are going. That'll go viral. Actually, don't do that. I'd rather keep out of it, really. BUT GO VIRAL! Whatever, just BE YOU."

This is why Danny and I work. He gets me and he gives me an ego turbo-boost. I sort of skip all the way to Granddad's house. It's not exactly a skip, as that would be highly embarrassing as I'm not actually seven, but it's a very positive stompy walk.

#CallTeresa

When I get to Granddad's house, Aunty Teresa answers the door. I ask her what she is doing. Rule number one for a calm life: NEVER ask Aunty Teresa what she is doing.

"Ermm. We are mostly doing goat noises and listing people we'd like on our dartboard of hate," she says, like it's the most totally normal thing in the world.

"And how does that work?" I ask. I never learn. Rule number two: Don't ask for details.

Aunty Teresa drags me into the front room. My dad is there standing over a homemade target, which has a big red bull's-eye marked THE WORST in the middle of it. He gives me a huge hug.

"Millie," he says proudly, "behold the greatest advance in stress relief ever! You simply pin all the things you can't stand onto this, and then you throw darts at it."

I read what Aunty Teresa and Dad have written on it.

- Noisy eaters
- People who post a sad face on Facebook so everyone writes "Are you okay, Hun?"—JUST TELL US WHAT IS ACTUALLY WRONG!

- People who walk slowly in the mall. I'm shopping. MOVE!
- Seahorses

"What's up with seahorses?" I ask.

Aunty Teresa looks at me like I've asked something incredibly stupid. "Well, you can't ride them, and all they do is float around looking pretty. I want more from my marine creatures. Look at sharks! They bring DRAMA!"

"But male seahorses can give birth!" I tell her. I've been googling a lot. Lauren and I have fact wars. This is mainly because Lauren thinks she can go on game shows with all her knowledge and become very rich very quickly. For her, the weirder the fact the better. The bizarre thing is, trivia also really helps me manage my stress. When my brain is worrying what the capital of Bhutan is, it's not full of anxiety about other stuff I can't control.

"Pregnant fish men! Fake news!" Teresa says. And I have to google this fact to prove it to her. She makes her "massively amazed" face where her nose accordions into her forehead and she practically dislocates her skull. "Right," she shouts, "seahorses are off and goats are back on."

My dad looks outraged and hollers, "NO! Think of the cheese!"

Aunty Teresa pounces on him and they start wrestling on the floor. They don't notice as I leave for the kitchen. Granddad is standing there mopping the floor. He seems like he's in another world. I say "Hi" to him, but he just carries on cleaning. I wave madly in his direction. When he's tuned out, this is the only thing that ever works.

"Oh, hello, superstar," he finally says. He's called me "superstar" since all this going-viral stuff happened. I don't really like it, but this is Granddad trying to be sweet. He doesn't normally believe in compliments. He thinks they make you arrogant and according to him there are few things worse than a "big-headed female." Yes, he is sexist as he's ancient and most people were back then. Women used to be sexist to themselves! I make allowances for my grandpa. He's family.

"Sorry, Millie," he says, "I was in a world of my own. I do my best thinking when I'm mopping. Once you are used to the nature of the job, your body does one thing and it frees your mind to ponder the complexities of the universe."

I give Granddad a cuddle. We are beyond words sometimes, especially when he goes too deep.

"I expect you've come around to get your things. So you're leaving me with these two fools?"

At that point I hear Teresa yell, "PUT MUSHROOMS BACK ON THE DARTBOARD OF HATE. They are EVIL. It's like eating moldy mini umbrellas."

Granddad looks at me sadly. "I'll miss you, gal. I will miss you."

We have an uncomfortable moment. This is because Granddad doesn't really do feelings. He gets emotional and then changes the subject to the first thing that pops into his head before you have a chance to react.

"Nothing wrong with mushrooms!" he shouts at Teresa. "Well, except the ones that can kill you."

He looks at me and winks. "Would you like to use my shed for one of your things before you go? For old times' sake?"

I've been using Granddad's shed as my vlog spot. I'd sort of hoped he'd let me keep on using it, but I think he wants his man cave back and, as I hear Teresa and my dad fighting over murder fungi, I kind of understand that. It's good to have a place to hide in life.

I put my arm around Granddad's shoulder and give him a kiss. He grabs his mop and pretends to attack me with it. That's one of the ways he tells me he loves me.

Families are weird, aren't they? All families. I've never met a normal one.

THIS IS A BOOK ABOUT YOUR BRAIN
AND HOW TO LOOK AFTER IT.

fiercereads.com